Thorn's Bride

Stefanie Lassitter

PublishAmerica
Baltimore

First printing

ISBN: 1-4137-5232-2
PUBLISHED BY PUBLISHAMERICA, LLLP
www.publishamerica.com
Baltimore

Printed in the United States of America

~ To Marc, my husband and loyal friend ~

Special thanks to Christy A. Byce, Lovells Historical Society, and Pastor Art Larson and the congregation of Tri-Lakes Baptist Church of Brighton, Michigan.

All have been wonderfully influential in the development of this book.

Prologue

September, 1872

Phyllida waved to her friends and students until the carriage rounded the bend and they could no longer be seen. She leaned against the window and sighed. Saying good-bye was hard for Phyllida, and as she passed the sign "Pritchard School for Girls," she fought the surfacing tears. She would particularly miss Ada Pritchard, the school's headmistress and founder. Ada had become Phyllida's confidante and friend after she joined the school as a student nearly six years before. Phyllida liked Ada's vivacious spirit and her strong commitment to the education of less fortunate girls.

When Phyllida's Aunt Chloe died, her aunt's husband, Ernst, immediately arranged for Phyllida to attend school. They had little money despite Ernst's job as a solicitor for a wealthy family. Ernst himself came from money and was linked to Langworthy Lumber, a prominent family whose fortune was established in America. He knew little of his cousins, the Langworthys, but found that having the same last name brought him the prestige he enjoyed. Unfortunately, among Ernst's enjoyments was that of spending money. Ernst had a tab everywhere and when his debts mounted higher and higher, he borrowed money to pay his creditors. One time he confided in Chloe,

"I'm robbing Peter to pay Paul." Chloe despised such extravagances and begged him to stop, even pawning jewelry and other trinkets to keep creditors at bay. When Chloe died he was up to his ears in debts, and was barely able to pay for Chloe's burial. Phyllida took over Chloe's role as housekeeper, and worrier. She too scraped to make ends meet, often pawning her own heirlooms from her mother. Ernst thought highly of Phyllida, but was uncertain what to do with the girl. Phyllida, he thought, was a delicate beauty like her mother, Chloe's sister. He knew he could secure his future and hers by marrying her off. Phyllida was smart, pretty and very talented in singing. Her only irritating trait, he once remarked to Chloe, was her shyness. This, along with financial despair, made it impossible to bring her into London society where girls of her status began their journey to marriage.

Chloe made Ernst promise her that he would care for Phyllida. He consented; uncle and niece lived together peacefully. He tried to stay away from the gambling clubs, while Phyllida cooked, cleaned, and educated herself by reading mountains of books. Meanwhile, Ernst's debts were still there and his reputation was sullied, since he owed money everywhere. He was forced to sell the home, his beloved possessions, the last of Chloe's jewelry—a fact that left him sick to his heart—and her dresses, though they were slightly outdated. He remembered the way Phyllida suppressed her tears as she watched her dead aunt's wardrobe being packed and sent away. Within a month of Chloe's death, they were homeless and penniless. He was feeling the brunt of his failing career since no one wanted a solicitor with the reputation of having extravagant debts. His cousin, Edward Langworthy, sent him enough money to get by, but soon he dried up that financial well by repeatedly borrowing without repayment. Edward's letters expressed disappointment and regret, and soon their brief correspondence ended.

With the last little bit of money, he sent Phyllida to a small, inexpensive school outside London called Pritchard School for Girls. He was assured that Phyllida's room and board were secure before turning his attention to finding employment. Phyllida later discovered that Ada had accepted her into the school despite her uncle's inability to consistently keep the school bills paid. When Phyllida was hired on as a music teacher, she tried to persuade Ada to let her repay what her uncle had owed, but Ada would not hear of it. She would always remember Ada's tall, willowy figure, her hair pulled back into a severe bun at the nape of her neck, as her thin arms grasped each elbow. She looked every inch of the spinster she had become, and even the first impression she gave was that of a bitter, ornery schoolmarm—until she smiled. Her smile, wide and bright, chased away first impressions. She loved the Lord and her students. Without Ada, Phyllida thought, she herself would be unsaved and lost, for it was Ada who led Phyllida to the Lord. Phyllida experienced the Lord's love and for the first time in her life, she experienced hope, joy and a peace beyond her understanding. She tried to share this experience to Ernst in a letter, since he never visited her. He did not reply nor did he communicate with her again until his death.

Ernst's eventual death followed by the raw truth of his financial ruin touched Phyllida in a very significant way, changing her life and her future forever. The carriage took her further away from Pritchard School for Girls and drew her closer to America, a great, unfathomable place where she would meet Uncle Ernst's family, the Langworthys.

Chapter 1

Autumn in Michigan meant muddy roads and a flooded Au Sable River. But Thorn Langworthy didn't mind. The heavier the river currents, the quicker the logs traveled south to the Great Lakes. Soon the roads and riverbanks would be icy, making log transportation easier.

The wilderness had been ravaged by rains and overworked lumberjacks. Not one tree stood as far as he could see. He paused to regard a fallen tree drug by a tired Belgian horse team. The men, covered in mud, sweat, and autumn rains, shivered slightly, exhaling white puffs of steam. Irving Hamilton, the camp's foreman, walked wearily alongside Thorn. "My men need a break, sir. They've pushed fourteen hours with one lunch break."

Thorn hesitated. Irving ran his hand through his red hair and put his hat back on. Mud and sawdust found its way into his thick red moustache and eyebrows. Thorn glanced up at the sky. "We have two more hours of good daylight, Hamilton."

That's all he needed to say. No one argued with Thorn Langworthy. The last man who had protested found himself hobbling to the train station to purchase a one-way ticket out of Lovells. Rumor had it that Thorn had threatened to kill him if he came across county lines.

Thorn could do that considering he owned the county line.

Thorn, as usual, wore an immaculate white shirt, black tie and gray suit. He was a gentleman even in the filthiest surroundings. His black leather gloves strained across his large hands as he clasped his notes and pencil. "I want a log count by day's end, Hamilton."

"Yes, sir." He walked away, his heels slightly sinking, yet Thorn Langworthy remained untouched by the thick black mud. A group of lumberjacks once remarked that mud just didn't stick to Thornton Langworthy.

"Why is that?" one had asked.

"I see it like this," the veteran lumberjack said as they exchanged stories around the fire. "Snakes don't get muddy because they're so cold and slippery. That's Thornton Langworthy for ya."

Lewis, who had been waiting in the trap, greeted his brother. "Dinner starts in twenty minutes."

"Dinner doesn't start until I'm home," Thorn said casually as he alighted the trap.

Wisely Lewis didn't reply. Lewis Langworthy, the youngest of the three brothers, resembled his brother with dark hair and dark eyes, but he was considerably shorter. He never got used to his older brother having twice his strength and height. He noticed the way Thorn's long legs hung out of the trap and his wide shoulders nearly shoved him aside. "All of Papa's traits are wasted on you," Lewis used to tell his brother. "You don't care a bit about women, just about money."

To Thorn, money was more predictable and easier to manage. "There's nothing I hate more than a silly woman," he often said. The last time he was involved with a woman, he found himself leaving Wisconsin, breathing a sigh of relief. Thoughts of Clarice Moss made him shiver. "Like I always say," he sneered with bitterness, "a silly woman attracts a silly man; two idiots are bad news."

Once Lewis pulled the trap away from naked land, they traveled the narrow road towards Twin Pines, their home on Shupac Lake. The home, built in the manner of a small Georgian estate, seemed slightly out of place among the thick Michigan forest. They rounded the bend, both men silent as if seeing Twin Pines for the first time. The white Georgian mansion boasted tall windows, rectangular in shape, which reached gracefully toward the square roof. A modest, yet immaculate, garden trimmed the drive and loitered around the front of the house. Thorn's father had the home built to resemble the childhood estate he had left behind in England. Thorn vaguely remembered the rolling English estate. Rather, his most vivid memories of England consisted of his mother crying as his father explained that selling Langworthy Hall was an investment. "To start again in America, Jenna, has been a dream of mine. Don't let me down." He remembered his mother reluctantly nodding in submission.

She was never happy in America. His father profited beautifully, buying nearly all the land in Crawford County and half in each existing neighboring county. They were rich, immensely rich. Why wouldn't that have pleased his mother? She liked Michigan, but she loved England. Though northern Michigan resembled England in some respects, it wasn't enough. Mother died nearly eight years later while his father was at the peak of his success. What a time to leave Father, Thorn thought bitterly. But as the years sped by, Thorn was less bitter towards his mother. There were times when he actually missed her kindness, her soft touch and loving voice. But before such sentimentalities could rob him of common sense, he threw himself into work. Soon his mother was nothing more than a fragment of his past, small and somewhat insignificant.

Lewis, on the other hand, loved his mother and bawled like a baby when she died. Even as they neared Twin Pines, Lewis remarked, "Mother would have loved the flowerbeds. Look at how her mums still come up every year. All thirty-seven of them."

"You counted the mums, Lewis?" Thorn asked, glancing at his brother with disdain.

"Don't start, Thorn," he said, knowing this would begin another tirade of how he was still tied to the apron strings, and how he would have been wiser to exercise his counting on coppers rather than on a silly flowerbed.

Thorn sighed as Edith, the head housekeeper, met him at the door. She waited as Thorn removed his gloves and hat. "Is dinner ready?" he greeted her.

"Yes sir. Mr. Sanford is waiting for you and Mr. Lewis."

"Tell Sandy I'll be down in a moment," Thorn said as his eyes lingered on the grand staircase. He loved the house and in four months he hoped the house would be his and only his. He traced his hand along the carved oak staircase. He remembered how his father had tried to convince his mother what a beautiful piece of furniture it was. "It's real oak, Jenna, not like the black medal railings at Langworthy Hall."

But his mother was unimpressed. Why couldn't she just have been happy with Twin Pines? Instead she tried reminding her sons that there was more to life than material things. Sandy and Lewis ate out of her hand, but Thorn rarely bought it; there was a time when he too connected with his mother's teachings about God.

But that was history.

He truly felt satisfied when Father rewarded him for his tireless efforts. "No one works harder than you, Thorn. You will turn Langworthy Lumber into an empire—everything that it should be." It was true. Langworthy Lumber dominated demand and supply in the Midwest. Hundreds of men worked in camps throughout the Upper and Lower Peninsulas and in northern Wisconsin. He loved what it became. The dream would never have materialized had his father not sold Langworthy Hall. "You're selling your childhood, your upbringing, and even your integrity!" his mother often cried. But Thorn's father dreamed of more. He wanted a larger estate, more land, more horses…

Thorn washed for dinner and changed his shirt. Like his father, he always required family to wear clean shirts as dinner at Twin Pines was a formal affair. His brothers were drinking coffee in the drawing room when he entered. Without a word, Thorn curtly motioned and the brothers put down their cups and followed him into the dining room. A wide chandelier glittered over the immaculate setting and he once again appreciated his father's taste and insistence for exquisite décor and fine white linen. A mahogany buffet lined one wall where various pastries were set. On the other wall, two of his mother's favorite oil paintings hung. The windows themselves overlooked Shupac Lake.

Thorn watched Sandy's head bent in earnest prayer noting his brother's light hair and olive skin. He had taken after their mother, where Thorn and Lewis were dark like their father. When Sandy finished praying, they looked to Thorn who nodded mutely to be seated. Dinner began.

Edith's daughters, Annie and Bella, stood in attendance refilling glasses and taking away dirty linen. A guest once remarked how formal their customs were, especially for bachelors in remote northern Michigan. But Thorn had replied, "It's tradition." Tradition to Thorn was the bulwark of life. Anything out of the ordinary just wouldn't do. Yet recently, his father had left parting words that would completely turn his life upside down, and Sandy wasted no time in getting to the matter.

"Have you heard from our English cousin?" he asked.

"Yes, and she has accepted the terms of employment," Thorn replied flatly.

"What 'terms of employment'? And when is she coming?" Lewis asked.

Thorn set down his fork. "Phyllida Cowen is en route to America as we speak. She will telegram when she arrives in New York. Which reminds me," he said, turning to Annie who was slicing the beef. "See that fresh flowers are taken to Miss Cowen's room."

Annie nodded and Sandy said, "You didn't answer Lewis's question, Brother. I'd be very curious to know to what 'terms of employment' you're referring."

"She's coming in the capacity of an employee."

"What? Do you mean as a lumberjack?" Lewis nearly laughed. "She doesn't know that you plan to propose marriage to her?"

Thorn didn't reply and Sandy spoke up. "Before he died, Papa told you to take a year to travel abroad. He said you were overworked and lonely. You were supposed to temporarily relocate to England, re-establish your roots and find a bride in the process. Those were Papa's intentions. Now you've sent for a bride as you would send for a piece of merchandise from a catalog!"

"You ignored his dying wishes." Lewis stabbed at the roast beef.

"I don't need either of you to lecture me," Thorn said. "I know what must be done. The last thing my schedule can afford is a silly trip to England. Besides, the whole idea of marrying against my wishes has not rested well with me. I'm not the marrying kind."

"And what do you do if she also isn't the marrying kind?" Sandy asked. "Shouldn't you have looked into this sooner?"

"She'll marry me," Thorn said with confidence.

Sandy ignored him and went on, "You've got a few months left and Twin Pines, the whole business, land…everything, will be held up in court. Papa was very specific that you should have it all and not us."

"And you can't forgive him for that, can you?" Thorn asked pointedly as he handed Annie the plate of butter. "I like butter rolled in parsley. This will not do."

Annie left and he turned back to Sandy who was saying, "I've never wanted this," as he waved his hand. "I'd be just as happy living in a small cabin rather than inherit this dragon."

Thorn believed him and relaxed a little. Sandy wasn't interested in material things. He did his job well, complained little, and maintained a life involved in church. Though he thought Sandy was foolish, he privately respected him for his beliefs. Lewis said, "Papa still could have considered me in his will."

"Listen to yourselves," Thorn sneered, "you still refer to him as 'Papa.' He became 'Father' to me years ago. Besides, Father left you several acres to do with what you wish. Why don't you build a house or something?"

"Maybe one day I will. It has always been a dream of mine," Lewis said. "You're the one with the fortune, not I."

"It's not his fortune yet," Sandy said. "I don't care a whit for it all, but at least I want to see someone in the family inherit it. I'd like to see Papa's wishes acknowledged, no matter how unusual they seem."

"Now, back to the matter of your bride. Have you really done an extensive search?" Lewis asked.

"I haven't had the time or the interest. That's why I enlisted Ronnie's help." Veronica, a close neighbor and friend, looked out for the three brothers as if they were her own sons. She prided herself on speaking her mind and furnishing everyone she knew with her pearls of wisdom. Thorn liked Veronica because she was direct, pleasant and so unlike the flighty women he had known in his life.

"Well, she tried to help you. Didn't she bring over three lovely British girls? And look how you treated them," Sandy recalled with mild embarrassment.

"Those girls were silly. One fluttered her eyelashes and pawed at my sleeves; I had to remind her that she was not courting me."

"As I recall," Lewis said lightly, "she left in tears saying 'good riddance.'" He pulled a face mimicking a crying woman by batting his eyelashes and thrusting his lips. In a high-pitched voice he said with a perfect British accent, "You're so horribly cruel, Thornton Langworthy."

Thorn smiled; he never laughed.

"You make light of something quite serious— " Sandy said, his face flushed.

"I'm not interested in marriage; I have no idea why Father did this to me."

"I know very well why he did— " Sandy countered and Thorn held up his hand.

"I don't care to discuss it," he said, his already thin patience coming to an end.

"You let greed get the better of you and it killed Father…" He was clenching his napkin watching Thorn with distaste. His honest, wide blue eyes reminded Thorn of his mother.

"Stop!" He slammed his fist on the table, making the china jolt. Annie, who was walking in with the butter, jumped and dropped the dish. "Clean that up or I'll have you replaced by the end of the week! And you," he thundered at Sandy, "don't ever bring up Father's death to me again."

"You're a bigger fool than I realized," he said coolly.

"Go run to your Bible. I don't need your preaching here in my house."

"It's not your house yet, Thorn."

Thorn noticed Sandy didn't call him "Brother," an indication of his fury.

"Look, the girl will marry me. I've paid Cousin Ernst's debts. She is probably relieved and flattered by my generosity. How she would have eventually paid for the fool's debts is beyond me."

"What do you know of her?" Lewis asked, glancing at Annie who was cleaning the last of the broken butter tray.

"She's become some kind of music teacher at a ladies' school. I assume she is a bit older, educated and without a husband."

"Why didn't you tell us about this?" he asked.

Thorn shrugged. "I find this whole matter of minimal importance. But as Sandy mentioned, we're nearing the anniversary of Father's death and I still don't have a British wife."

"I suppose it seems like a good plan," Lewis consented.

"Ernst's solicitor gave me the idea. He had pity on Miss Cowen's debt and indicated to me the amount owed. I wished to aid our dear cousin-by-marriage. So, I wrote a cheque to the solicitor to cover the debt and then a letter to Miss Cowen. In return I asked her to come to Michigan for employment at my estate."

"That's a bit deceptive, Brother," Lewis said.

"You can interpret it any way you please, but I nearly have this cat in the bag."

"Is that just a cliché, or are you referring to the girl?" Sandy asked, mildly disgusted.

Thorn didn't answer as he was used to Sandy's constant disapproval.

Lewis asked, "What if she's horribly fat and missing teeth?"

"Who cares? I want a wife to claim what's rightfully mine. If I find her nature incredibly despicable, I can employ her to work here in some capacity and continue my search for a wife. That way," he turned to his self-righteous brother, "she was not deceived at all."

"But your foremost plan is to marry her," Sandy said flatly.

"Right away and without question," he said, curtly slicing the buttered potatoes.

"What if she won't have you?"

"A lonely little music teacher from England?" he said. "She wouldn't dare. What kind of woman would refuse lands, an endless bank account and a wardrobe full of dresses for every day of the year?"

"Women want more than that," Sandy warned, remembering his mother's unhappiness.

Ignoring his exasperated brother, Thorn asked, "What woman doesn't want marriage?"

The ship rocked with such force that the gaslights hanging on the rusted hooks swayed with violence. One man grabbed a lantern to steady the oil that splattered the hovering passengers.

Together the frightened passengers of *The Mermaid* huddled in the bowels of the creaking ship. Phyllida had never traveled by ship—nor did she ever plan to again. She felt ill, but not so much from the motion of the ship as the odor that permeated the ventless room. The smell of vomit and urine, assumably from sickness and fear, caused her to reach for her smelling salts. The dark room and swaying lights threw shadows over the passengers' weary faces. She saw women crying and clutching their children while clinging to the wall, as if the ship's walls could save their lives. The men seemed equally as nervous but appeared reserved with white, taunt faces. The mixture of dialects and languages made communication difficult. While one man shouted in French, another replied in frightened Russian. However, their goals were the same: to reach America safely.

"America," Phyllida sighed. She often imagined what America was like with its endless wheat fields, woodlands, lakes and deserts. America embodied all climates and all cultures. Now she was going to be a part of it, all because of God's grace. She reached for one of Thorn's letters and by the swaying lights she read it again and again. It was really true.

He offered her employment to America. His second letter was promptly sent but did not provide further details of her new position. Instead, he sent a one-way ticket on *The Mermaid* as well as enough money to pay her expenses from New York to Michigan. The letter expressed his delight at her acceptance. He went on to tell her about Michigan weather, the president and other odds and ends. However, he noted that he wished her to "telegram us upon your arrival to New York. I should like to know when you arrive—I do not care for surprises." She made a mental note and turned back to the hysteria that arose as the ship seemed to plummet further into the eye of the storm.

"We're going to die!" one woman cried, followed by the screaming of her children.

"Please be calm, everyone!" another spoke up. "Let's remain quiet. Can someone sing us a song to calm our nerves?"

The room was temporarily silenced despite the thunder outside. Phyllida's heart raced. For a moment, she was more frightened of singing in front of strangers than the angry storm that threatened to sink the ship! But she knew better. She had an opportunity to sing and offer comfort. She raised her trembling hand as the lantern swayed over her small, frightened face.

Phyllida made her way to the center of the room where she clutched a table that was bolted to the floor. She cleared her voice and breathed a quick, silent prayer. Then she began to sing "Great is Thy Faithfulness." At first her voice cracked with self-consciousness, then her voice, more mature than she appeared, reached firm, sounding heights. The smoothness and depth of her song seemed to overtake the room and a quiet silence settled therein. One passenger, sifting through his carpetbag, produced a tattered fiddle. Together they made music, she clutching the bolted table while he saddled the bench and gave his strength to playing and simply holding on for dear life.

Within minutes, the room came alive with music. People began to sing, and those who could not speak English hummed gospel hymns with reverential awe. The storm forgotten, the children calmed, and a group of people brought together all in God's name was lead in song by the small woman with the heavy gold hair and brown eyes.

Thorn rarely had a full night's sleep. Tonight would be no exception. He tossed and turned, moved in and out of sleep only to visit and re-visit the same dream. In the dream he found himself by a river as Clarice Moss pulled off the sapphire ring and threw it into the churning current. Her face never changed as she glared at him in hatred.

Then somewhere in the blurred dream, a baby cried.

He woke with a gasp.

The flame flickered mischievously around the room. He glanced at his face in the mirror and turned away in disgust. "I'm a grown man, but I let the same dream terrify me every night." This was one facet of his mind he could not control, but at least he had the ability to end the dream when the baby cried.

Thorn made his way to the library, his feet creaking along the corridors. The house was dark and silent as the full moon threw shadows across the foyer. Thorn paused to look up at the portrait of his father. The silvery light emphasized his father's dark, proud eyes. Thorn often looked at the portrait, thinking it was an incredible likeness. His father had had the self-portrait done ten years ago, while he was in his prime. He noted the way his father's strong hand rested on the lapel of his jacket. His proud chin, much like Thorn's, tilted upward showing what Veronica called his "blueblood snootiness." Perhaps she was right. His father, a proud descendent of earls and dukes, carried the similar streak of pride.

Tonight his father seemed to look down at him across the foyer with disdain, or a sort of impatience. "Buck up, my boy! Don't let dreams of babies and that Moss woman work you over!" The moonlight was deceptive. Was it his father of ten years ago laughing at him, or the pathetic dying man watching his son in pity? He made his way to the nook in the kitchens where he wasted no time lighting a small fire. Though the autumn night was warm, he liked the crackle and smell of a homey fire. The small room, adjacent to the kitchens, had a small grate, two chairs and a window that overlooked the lake. His father had had the nook built for Edith, who liked to have a small place to sit with her daughters rather than the large, drafty kitchen. Thorn took a liking to the spot as it brought comfort.

When he had enough light, he pulled the letter from his housecoat.

Thorn had read the letter three times.

The only occasions he took the time to read anything thrice was to proofread his cheques. But Miss Phyllida Cowen's letter piqued his interest.

He fingered the envelope, noting the fine feminine script. He was struck by her use of words, and the way she formed her sentences. She was presumably educated and tolerably charming, he thought. He considered few women to be charming. He often watched Lewis swoon when a woman flirted, but Thorn called it utter manipulation. There was nothing sweet or enticing about a silly girl who batted her eyelashes or rested her hand on a man's arm. He had once fallen victim to such tomfoolery. After his relationship with Clarice Moss, he ceased admiring pretty women. He was graced with shrewdness and good financial judgment. He could smell a phony a mile away and as a result, when he walked into crowded room, he didn't see the colorful gowns, sparkling diamonds and pretty smiles. He saw other men in suits who would need his lumber—whether they yet realized it or not.

Of course there were times when he longed for a companion and friend. But what was a friend? He had never been a friend to anyone. In his father's later years, he seemed disinterested in his own company, and focused rather on getting Thorn a wife. He couldn't understand his father in those last years. Thorn shoved away thoughts of his father as his eyes lingered over the thin, rather cheap paper stamped "Pritchard School for Girls."

"…Sometimes I think the rains will never end. How I wish summer were here, waking us from our hibernation and sending us outside where true beauty lies. I just love to take the first walk of spring, to drink in the smell of fresh foliage, and yes, even the faint scent of rotting leaves in the brook…"

Phyllida Cowen didn't ramble, discussing frocks, hairstyles, or who's who of London. She obviously had never had a mentor to help her "come out," as they said in London society. Perhaps she was homely, or slightly fat, like Lewis had cautioned. But he didn't particularly care. To Thorn, beauty failed to succumb to the same definition as it did for most men. He watched Lewis pant over girls whose dresses and heavy makeup looked like they belonged on a wedding cake. No, he didn't quite know how to picture Miss Phyllida Cowen. He didn't like that either. He needed the control of a mental picture, something to prepare him for meeting her.

"...by the time you receive this letter late summer will have made its entrance and I shall be on my way to America. The timing was God-sent...there's no doubt God has opened a door..."

Phyllida had mentioned God, yet it didn't annoy him. She didn't seem self-righteous or pious. Rather, he sensed urgency mixed with relief. Her letter was gracious, thanking him and her God for this opportunity.

Marriage might not be as big an obstacle as he had thought.

Reaching the harbor in New York was a relief. She booked a room for the night in a modest hotel. She found the owner to be less than patient as she asked for her luggage to be taken to her room. She took dinner in the lobby where she sat in the corner and had a light "sup," as Americans said. She adapted to their version of coffee and couldn't help but smile when the waiter refilled her cup commenting, "That'll put some roar into your boar." She wasn't sure what it meant, but thought the saying was funny. Phyllida pictured Ada rolling her eyes at such a slang expression. She found herself listening to the various conversations throughout the lobby. She detected a European accent here and there, but mainly American accents dominated the communication. Americans talked through their nose, she thought. American men laughed loudly, slapping each other on the back, while American women shrilled in laughter and grasped each other's hands. She gathered Americans to be eager to talk about their feelings, touch one another and establish quick but fleeting friendships.

She wasn't sure about Americans.

Phyllida was glad to be back in the confines of her room. Had she made the wrong decision? Had she hastily blundered in her move to America? "Lord, I'm doubting myself. If You really have a goal for me, please give me a sense of peace." She curled in bed, hearing children playing games in the dark street below. Surprisingly, she slept immediately.

In the morning, she wrestled her way to the train depot, glancing nervously at the dray she had hired to transport her large trunk. At one point, a small dirty boy attempted to snatch her purse. She quickly shoved him away, but immediately regretted her hasty defense. An onlooker said, "Don't feel pity, ma'am. They're little thieves probably working for someone who takes care of them, no doubt." She carried on, the perspiration dampening her forehead. People crowded the New York depot, shoving and pressing toward unknown destinations. She finally tightened her shoulders and moved forward, caring less and less about politeness. For a moment she watched the chaos surrounding a taxi that had collided with a vegetable stand. Children scattered to grab food while the merchant and the driver shouted at each other. She had never heard such colorful language nor had she ever experienced such a difficult city. In high windows, people watching the turmoil hollered their version of the accident. Others watched with curiosity while pulling in their laundry that hung between buildings. Many people looked starved and disheveled and openly begged for "alms for the poor."

Phyllida heard the hiss of the train engine and gave her ticket to the conductor. When she was shown her coach seat, she collapsed, removed her hat and leaned her head against the cool window. Just as the train sluggishly moved forward, she gasped, "The telegram!" She had completely forgotten to send the Langworthys a telegram! She bit her lip and sighed; it was all too overwhelming! Somehow she pictured America to be a sort of colony, clean and orderly. She had looked at a sketching in her book of pretty Boston homes, shiny carriages and clean, happy people. New York, as a first impression of America, certainly fell short of her romantic expectations.

The next day the train pressed on to Michigan. She had napped and enjoyed a meal consisting of bread and cheese. After feeling recovered from her harrowing New York experience, she turned her attention to the scenery. Northern Michigan was like northern England in several respects, but she was surprised by the population of pines. Thick massive pine trees dominated the landscape. Occasionally she saw farmlands and a few towns, but the trees ruled the views. She opened the window and drank in the pungent, warm scent of the trees. She liked Michigan already. Summer was maturing into early fall. Orange, fire red, and bright yellow leaves danced on the maple and oak trees, as the cool crisp air filtered into her compartment along with the faint aroma of a wood fire burning in the distance. She yearned to get off the rambling train and begin to explore her new world.

She must have dozed again for when she awoke, the noon sun was slanting boldly into the window. The train slowed and she peered at the barren, horrible land. Pine trees were being dragged away by the bundles. Thin, gaunt men hacked weakly at trees as tired horses marched slowly, dragging more than their share of logs. As the train moved on, she saw ramshackle tents where dirty, thin men sat and ate slowly. A larger tent housed long tables where cooks spooned a watery substance into tin dishes. Few men glanced at the passing train, instead focusing on nothing, their gazes inscrutable.

"That's a sorry sight," said a woman's voice.

Phyllida jumped and the young woman cried, "Forgive me, you must have thought you were alone. We saw you were sleeping and crept in."

"I think you've frightened her," her male companion laughed.

Phyllida waved aside their apologies. "No bother. Was that a kind of prison camp we just passed?"

"No," the young man answered, "but it looks like one. It's a lumber camp."

"Those men work in such conditions of their own free will?" she asked incredulously.

"There isn't a great deal of work these days," the girl murmured sympathetically. Phyllida was saddened. She turned to glance outside and was met once again with thick pines, as if the scene had never existed. The girl had been watching her and asked, "How far north are you headed?"

"A small town named Lovells, outside of Grayling," she answered.

"Ah," the man said, "into more of Langworthy country, I see."

"Yes, that's who I'm meeting, a Mr. Thornton Langworthy."

The couple turned wide-eyed as if seeing her for the first time. The young lady asked cautiously, "Are you going to Twin Pines?"

Phyllida recalled the return address on Mr. Langworthy's letter. "Yes, that's right. Is Twin Pines the name of the Langworthys' home?"

"It's more like the name of their estate. Are you a relative?"

Phyllida immediately got the impression that the Langworthys were wealthy. The two newcomers judged by Phyllida's very used coat that she was either a poor relation or an employee. She explained that she was coming to work for the family. She noticed the young man, who had introduced himself as Alfred, nudge his fiancée, Esther. Yet Esther didn't notice his attempt to refrain her questions.

"In what capacity are you working for the family? There are no children that would require a governess, and you certainly don't look like housekeeping staff..."

"Esther— " Alfred whispered.

"There are no children?" she asked. She had pictured Thornton Langworthy as a married man with several children.

But before Esther could answer, the train was slugging to a stop. As Phyllida peered out the window, she thought she heard Alfred whisper, "That must be Thorn's bride."

Phyllida turned to question his statement, but the couple hurriedly stood and bid her farewell. Esther grasped her hands and peered earnestly into Phyllida's eyes, "Good luck to you, Miss."

Her sincerity struck Phyllida. It was as if she were saying she would really need it.

Phyllida was charmed by Lovells.

She stepped into the depot, and her luggage was ushered into a small sitting room. She looked around, pleased with her surroundings.

Across the tracks and down the road, a restaurant called Ruby's advertised huckleberry pie topped with fresh cream for five cents. Small shops such as a gift shop, butcher shop, bakery and a dress shop called Maisy's lined the uneven dirty road. She listened to several men discussing pay cuts and threatening to quit the lumber business. Before she could further eavesdrop, a gentleman who had been watching her stepped forward.

"Excuse me, Miss. You seem a bit lost. May I help you?"

Phyllida stared at him with uncertainty and he laughed. "I'm the station master here. It's sort of my job to see that all passengers make their way home safely. I haven't seen you in these parts before. Where are you headed?"

She smiled, unaware of a group of women watching her curiously. "Forgive me. I'm a bit weary from travel. I'd like to hire a trap to take me to Twin Pines."

The manager stared for a moment as if not understanding. Thinking that her accent might be too thick and confusing, she said carefully, "Perhaps I should be more specific. I need to hire a trap to take me to the Langworthy estate."

The station seemed to come to a temporary halt. The women stared wide-eyed, this time catching Phyllida's attention. A couple of men ceased hauling luggage to hear the conversation. Phyllida turned crimson.

"Of course, Twin Pines..." he stammered. "Let me show you to our sitting room and I'll summon a trap for you. Mr. Langworthy usually sends the family carriage. Does he know you're coming?"

"He had asked me to telegram when I arrived in New York, but I forgot. So no, I suppose they don't know I'm coming."

"I see. I'll take care of you promptly. Come this way."

As she entered the small sitting room, she thought she heard, for the second time, someone whisper, "That must be Thorn's bride."

"May the Lord watch over her," the other replied.

Chapter 2

"There's still no telegram. She probably hasn't reached New York yet," Sandy said.

The brothers had finished dinner and were drinking coffee with their neighbor Veronica Gray. She was slim, with red hair and deep red cheeks. She always wore red or burgundy. Though some would consider her attire a bit brash, the Langworthy men liked her confidence and bold manner. Thorn had been thinking again of Phyllida's letter when Lewis asked, "Are you certain you asked her to telegram us?"

Thorn nodded. "I'll be put out if she neglected to do as I asked."

"Oh Thorn, you may have to be 'put out' with this one. She's your last hope. If she refuses to marry you, you'll have to set out to England and find a bride yourself. There obviously aren't many in Michigan," Veronica reminded him.

"I expect orders to be followed, Ronnie. I made the point twice in my letter that she would need to telegram us when she reached New York. What if she is in Lovells right now wondering what to do?"

"If she's smart enough to travel to American, then she's smart enough to find her way to this little town," Veronica said. "I don't think that's your greatest worry."

"She's right," Sandy interjected. "You need to focus on how you will get her to marry you. You're down to just a few months before everything is turned over to the state."

Thorn didn't like the thought of strangers inhabiting the house, roaming about his properties. It made him shiver.

"She will marry me, I'm sure."

Veronica laughed, "My dear boy—yes, I will always think of you as my boy so don't dart that foul glance at me. You need to woo this young woman. You cannot command her to shove on a ring and sign a paper. Miss Cowen will need to know she can trust you."

"Get her to fall in love with you," Lewis' head was always in the clouds.

"Love?" Thorn sneered. "Don't be ridiculous. I haven't the time for such nonsense. Why, I have my hands full enough as it is trying to keep fires at bay, running the mill and making sure my men don't kill each other. Just the other day, camp twelve off Lewiston Point broke into an all-out fist fight. Irving Hamilton broke it up in time, but I've temporarily lost two men to a fractured jawbone and broken hand."

"What started the rumble?" Sandy asked.

"Hamilton said it began over low wages and heavy hours. I told him that was hogwash."

"Irving's right, Thorn. The men are discontent with the heavy hours you've put on them this last year. Then cutting their wages like you did really made things a nightmare," Sandy said.

"That's Hamilton's problem, not mine. If he can't make these fools behave, then I'll get rid of him and find someone more able." Of course it was a lot to expect Sandy to side with Thorn; he was always for underdogs like Irving Hamilton.

"You do that and the whole operation will collapse in front of you. Irving is the best man you've got here. He just gets under your skin because he's a devoted Christian." Sandy and Hamilton had been friends for years. It was not uncommon for Hamilton to witness to strangers and invite people to church. Thorn hated his boldness, and resented Hamilton's odd commitment to God. He thought Sandy and Hamilton to be two peas in a pod.

"He's either devoted or just plain odd, call it what you want. But the point is, I'm not interested in falling in love, not now, not ever."

"My boy, you're in for a long, bumpy ride. I just hope Miss Phyllida Cowen isn't the least bit opinionated or strong, for your sake, or you two are sure to lock horns. You mustn't assume all women are pliable and flimsy, and easy to mold into shape," Veronica said with her usual boldness.

"I'll manage her, whatever she's like," he said, leaving them.

"Don't count on it," Veronica laughed.

Phyllida was glad to have left the train station.

Whatever their thoughts, the townsfolk were unusually interested in Phyllida. She wanted to ask why the curious reception, but the driver was quiet, almost as if he was intimidated. She had heard the stationmaster tell the driver to bring her quickly and efficiently to Twin Pines.

Phyllida was feeling wary of the Langworthys.

"How well do you know the Langworthys?" she asked the young man, who drove nervously into a ditch when she spoke.

"I see them come and go from town," he answered curtly.

"What are their names? I suppose I should know my employer's names." She smiled, trying to warm him to her.

"There is Mr. Thorn, Mr. Sanford, and Mr. Lewis."

"Are they married?"

He glanced at her nervously. "Well, not yet."

"I see. Is one betrothed?"

"I don't know, Miss," he replied, this time turning around to look at her as if she should be the one to know such information.

She decided to stop prying and sit back. The trap rambled into the dense forest and the bright sunlight was hidden behind the thick pines. The path was quiet and peaceful. Suddenly she heard a low growl. She peered around. "What was that?

The horse reared slightly. "Whoa, Jack. Take it easy, boy. It sounds like a cougar. They're all over these parts."

"Oh my!" She clenched her hands.

"They're pretty shy creatures. Just as long as you don't wander around, poking behind fallen logs." He laughed lightly. "My pa says they're more scared of you than you are of them."

"My aunt used to say that about spiders," she said.

"There aren't cougars where you're from?"

"No." She shivered as she thought of a pair of unseen eyes watching them. She would have to quickly get used to the wilderness compared to the confines and comfortable routine of the quiet English boarding school.

"We're approaching Twin Pines, Miss."

Phyllida gaped at the large Georgian manor that loomed beside a lake. The white-washed house and arched windows looked like a common manor in England. She felt less homesick. "What a beautiful house," she cried as she noticed the bright mums lining a small pretty garden. She guessed a feminine hand loving nurtured the autumn flowers. The driver hastily came to a halt and helped her down. He set her trunks by the front door and rang.

She handed him a few coins, saying, "I hope I tipped you well. I am still unsure of the money here."

He didn't glance at his sizeable tip, but said, "I wish you and Mr. Thorn a great deal of happiness."

"I beg your pardon…"

The front door opened and a small, round woman greeted, "May I help you, Miss?"

"I'm Phyllida Cowen. I'm sure you're not expecting me…"

The woman's face flushed slightly. "Miss Cowen?" Her gaze assessed the small, petite girl with heavy gold hair.

"I'm afraid I've seen that bewildered expression a lot recently. Perhaps if I could see Mr. Thornton Langworthy…" she said politely, but feeling exasperated.

She stepped inside as two men walked from the drawing room. Moments later, a tall, older woman with red hair joined them in the foyer. Phyllida shyly introduced herself, all the while resenting the deep crimson flush that stained her face.

"Miss Cowen, so pleased to meet you. I'm Lewis Langworthy, and this is my brother Sanford, but everyone calls him Sandy."

His brother stepped forward, he too flushing, and shook hands. The resemblance between the brothers were vague, yet there was a similar, shared expression that she could not interpret. The red- headed woman laughed. "You must forgive us for our lack of manners. I'm Veronica, a friend of the family and their closest neighbor."

Veronica put her arm around Phyllida. Such gestures between strangers were uncommon in England, but at the moment it seemed to comfort her. "Now you pick your jaws up, boys. Miss Cowen didn't come all the way from England to be stared at like some kind of apple tart. Come here, m'dear. This is Edith, the head housekeeper and the mastermind behind keeping Twin Pines running so efficiently. These are her daughters, Annie and Bella." She led her around and introduced her to the rest of the staff. At length, she grasped Phyllida's hands. "You must be tired and a bit hungry. Edith, is the Lilac Room prepared?"

"But shouldn't I meet with Mr. Langworthy to discuss my employment…"

"Not too fast, m'dear. Let's get you settled first."

Phyllida followed Edith up the stairs while the family watched her. She heard the darker man, Lewis, say, "Brother's in for a real treat. Did you imagine she'd be so lovely?"

She trembled slightly as she reached for another sip of the lemon tea Edith had brought her. Edith seemed polite, slightly reserved, yet very apprehensive. Phyllida didn't understand the affect her coming had on the household. She almost sensed a sort of hope or dependency, as if her presence would decide some unknown fate.

Edith asked, "How do you like your room?"

"It's absolutely lovely, but much more than I expected." The Lilac Room was beautiful, adorned in every shade of purple from plum to palest lilac. A wide, four-poster oak bed dominated the floor along with an oak mantelpiece and a small writing desk. She loved the modern toilet consisting of a sink and tub in the adjoining room. But what caught her attention was the large spray of dried eucalyptus in front of the light, frilly curtains. She commented on this to Edith who said, "I'm sorry we didn't have fresh flowers. As you know, everything that grows is temporarily out of season."

"I like eucalyptus, Edith, thank you." How unusual, she thought. Paid employees, no matter how needed they were, did not have large, ornate rooms with special-ordered flowers from their employer.

"Mr. Thorn should be home shortly. I'll draw a bath for you while you wait."

"Thank you, Edith."

When she returned, she gathered the tea things and said, "Mr. Thorn wasn't aware of your arrival."

Phyllida didn't catch Edith's gentle reprimand. "Oh yes, I had forgotten to send a telegram."

By Edith's expression, Phyllida realized she had erred and asked, "Will he be upset?"

She paused and drew a breath and said in a private whisper, "Just be strong, Miss. Don't let him bully you."

"I don't understand the affect this man seems to have on everyone."

"God sent you here, Miss. I don't want to see you run away too soon."

"Why thank you…I think."

Edith laughed, her polite reserve abandoned. "We're a somber bunch, Miss. Pay me no heed."

Phyllida took this as her cue to prepare herself for the interview. After Edith departed, she quickly bathed and dressed in a long gray skirt and white blouse. She pinned her small silver watch to her collar and flicked away a trace of lint on her cuffs. She piled her heavy, thick hair into a knot behind her head and added a small pearl to each ear. She loved her pearl earrings, her only pieces of jewelry besides the watch that hadn't been pawned to pay her uncle's debts. The dampness from the bath pulled small tendrils about her face. She stared in the mirror, wishing she hadn't pinched her cheeks so hard, as her face was already flushed from the warm bath. She paused to regard herself in the mirror.

Ada always said that a woman mustn't stare into the mirror as it was considered vain. "You must only look at yourself long enough to make adjustments. Anything more is just plain vanity." Ada had often counted to ten as the young girls would preen themselves before the mirror. Phyllida whispered under her breath, "seven...eight..." and paused to really examine herself. She wanted desperately to make the right impression on her prospective employer. She was no longer dressing and preening herself to be regarded by her students. Today she dressed for a different role. She looked at herself critically, fully aware that she was being vain. She was not beautiful, she thought. Once, the pastor's son had told her she was pretty. Was she pretty? It didn't matter, really. But it would be nice to be striking. She wasn't striking. She was small, very small. Her figure was petite, her waist very narrow and her hips slender. Her small feet, encased in shoes with heels too high, were hidden beneath her skirt. She had always wanted to be tall, but then she would really stand out. Phyllida hated standing out in a crowd as her face easily turned red every time attention was drawn to her. Her lips were full—too full, she thought. They looked pouty and sullen if she didn't smile. Her nose was small, further emphasizing her full lips. Her eyes were rather large beneath her arched eyebrows. She always wished she had been graced with thick, curly lashes, but her eyes were wide, dark and very practical. "You have an honest face," Ada often commented. Yes, she thought, she had an honest face. But beauty and honesty were rarely linked when describing a woman; rather, women were described as either pretty or not pretty. It was that simple. Beautiful literary heroines were rarely described: "She is strikingly kind!" or "What a practical lady!" Instead, one was often assessed by looks and dress first. Oh, it didn't seem fair.

She glanced at her plain outfit with slight disdain. She always felt insecure when meeting people for the first time. Living with Ada and her students all those years kept her comfortable and safe as she rarely went to town and met with people her own age. She very seldom met her pupil's parents because that was Ada's job. But today she didn't have Ada, or leadership over her students. She wasn't Miss Cowen, the music teacher. Today she was plain, little Phyllida Cowen.

For a moment, she paused. "Lord, I feel so unsure of myself. Help me to be content with who I am, and how you made me. Give me strength and peace within myself. I've never been confident and I have little to offer the Langworthys. Please allow me to make the right impression." Then, as if finalizing her external assessment, she finished counting, "...nine...and ten."

She made her way to the drawing room where Lewis and Veronica warmly greeted her. She was particularly drawn to Veronica. She admired her taste in clothing and her direct manner. Her spirits lifted when Veronica exclaimed, "My, you are a doll! How old are you?"

"Twenty-five," she said.

"And never married?"

"No ma'am."

"Do you have a sister for our dear Lewis here?"

Lewis flushed. "You'll have to pardon Ronnie. She prides herself on all kinds of candid conversations." They laughed lightheartedly but she still wished to ask questions about her employment. As if reading her thoughts, Lewis distracted her by showing her several books of interest. The drawing room opened into a large library. The polished, oak shelves hosted hundreds of books. She was delighted, thinking how Ada would have been asking Mr. Langworthy for book donations within minutes of introduction: "Nice to meet you, Mr. Langworthy. Do you suppose you could find it in your heart to part with this lovely set of encyclopedias? A busy, successful man like yourself rarely has time to thumb through them, not like my poor students..." Phyllida smiled at herself thinking of Ada's directness and determination to succeed. Thoughts of Ada Pritchard gave Phyllida a small dose of confidence.

At length, raised voices could be heard in the hallway. She unsteadily rose and Lewis and Veronica fell silent. She noticed Lewis shelf a book and pause as if waiting.

"I was sent to come home. What's happening?" a voice thundered.

After a moment of silence, the same voice replied even louder, "She's here?"

"In the library," the quieter voice replied, then urged, "be polite."

"But she sent no telegram," the other protested.

"It doesn't matter, Brother. Miss Cowen arrived safely and soundly."

"I don't like my orders neglected. I made it very clear— "

"Hush, she will hear you. Look, Thorn, whether you want to admit it or not, we need her. The fate of Langworthy Lumber depends completely on..." The voice trailed off into an inaudible whisper.

The door opened slowly as Sandy entered, nodding warmly to Phyllida. Behind him followed a taller gentleman. His shoulders, wider than she'd ever seen on a man, turned to slide through the half-opened door. His olive skin was tanned from hours in the sun, but it was his eyes that arrested Phyllida.

They were dark. Almost like bottomless pits, their expression was mute of feeling and compassion. She shivered slightly. He continued to watch her, those strange eyes loitering about her. She flushed slightly but squared her shoulders. "Mr. Thornton Langworthy, I presume?"

"You must be Phyllida Cowen." He didn't shake her hand.

Sandy grappled for conversation. "She said the trip only lasted a bit over a week. Transportation has certainly improved— "

"I trust you arrived safely?" he interrupted and she detected a lingering British dialect, but still his tone was unlike the thick city accents of her students. His was refined and polished, resembling the upper class Queen's English.

How could she describe Thornton Langworthy? He was just like his name, she mused. His cleft chin and thin lips seemed permanently set in an expression of disgust. His face, though appearing polite, seemed to have an eternal scowl as if he was preoccupied with thoughts far removed from the immediate.

"I did, thank you."

"I hope you found the transition from the New York harbor to the depot satisfactory?"

"I suppose." She wondered where this line of questioning was headed.

"Then do you care to explain why you failed to telegram us at Twin Pines?"

"I'm just so pleased she is finally here— " Veronica began.

"I'm waiting, Miss Cowen."

Phyllida tilted her head to regard him before drawing a deep breath. "I suppose I've inconvenienced you, Mr. Langworthy. I simply forgot to send the telegram. I do sincerely apologize."

"I don't care for my orders to be treated flippantly."

"Thorn— " Lewis began.

Her patience was ebbing and her flush deepened. "Of course, I regret my folly— "

"How could you forget? The request was made in writing—twice."

Sandy attempted to interject. "It was no trouble, Miss Cowen. Such things happen…"

"I'd like a clearer answer."

"I'm afraid, Mr. Langworthy," she said, her voice edging slightly, her smile fading, "there is no 'clearer answer' for you. Our ship, *The Mermaid*, was in grave danger of sinking because of a horrid swell over the Atlantic. I thought I would die during the three-day journey. Then upon my arrival to New York, I was unprepared for the populated streets and rude people. I've traveled so little in my life so I felt getting from one destination to another with little confusion to be my utmost concern. It has been a long, very long week, Mr. Langworthy. I sincerely beg your pardon," she said looking as weary as she sounded.

"Do you plan to disregard orders in the future?"

She had been pushed too far.

"I will do whatever I can to please you. However, if your 'orders' present a grave inconvenience to me, I highly doubt I shall be put out. So, no, I cannot promise to obey you on every matter. You treat me as if I'm your wife. I submit to you as my employer, nothing more."

Sandy went pale and Thorn's fists clenched. "I didn't summon you here to let you take advantage of my generosity."

"Generosity?" She laughed this time, drawing a sarcastic tone.

"I don't care for your sarcasm," Thorn rebuked but not without seeing Lewis turn to hide his grin.

Sandy looked sick. "Miss Cowen, I'm afraid my brother has been a bit— "

"Don't excuse me, Sandy. And you," he said, glaring at the small woman whose eyes blazed like fire and whose flushed cheeks smoldered with a passion he found somewhat intriguing, "are dismissed from your post."

"Easy, Thorn— " Veronica said quietly.

"What post?" She laughed. "I've been here two hours and I'm already dismissed? Have it your way, Mr. Langworthy. As Americans say, I'll be gone 'in no time.'"

She went to move past him and he said, "Need I remind you that I paid your uncle's debts?"

She spun around. "He was your blood relative, and just my relation by pathetic marriage to my aunt! He didn't deserve her." To her horror her eyes welded with tears.

"Oh my," Sandy murmured in disdain as Thorn rolled his eyes, murmuring something about hysterical women.

Her blood boiled and soon any self-control was absent. "Don't patronize me, Mr. Langworthy! You can find your own employees, but next time when you summon them from England—or who knows where—pretending to be the great benefactor, inform them how cold and calloused you really are!"

She fled upstairs through a haze of tears and found her way to the Lilac Room. She hurriedly began to pack what little she had set on her bureau. Veronica tapped on the door and let herself in. "Phyllida…" she began.

"I appreciate your kindness, but I cannot stay under the same roof with that man." She threw her traveling habit into the suitcase.

Within minutes she threw open the door and marched down the stairs. Veronica hustled after her. "Honey, I don't blame you for being angry, but won't you reconsider?"

She was touched by the older woman's sincerity, but didn't reply. She brushed aside the last of her tears and made for the door. Sandy was calling, "Miss Cowen, I beg you…"

She closed the door and continued down the drive, carrying the large suitcase. She would have to send for her trunk later. She didn't know where she was going and didn't care. She imagined the servants hanging out the windows watching her as she walked own the drive, her shoulders squared and absurdly proud.

Veronica bustled into the library as Sandy ran outside to catch Phyllida.

"What where you thinking, Thorn?" Veronica hissed. "Have you gone mad? How could you treat the girl like that?"

"I want my orders considered priority, Ronnie. She will not toy with me." Thorn was ashamed, but he was not about to turn back on his word.

"You must go after her. She's already down the drive!"

"Let her go then," he said, not meaning his words.

"You're a bigger fool than I thought," Veronica said quite seriously. "I was always proud of you, Thorn. You brought your father much joy. But in the end of his life, he grew discouraged with you, your lust after the company, and this desire to own every inch of Michigan. He wanted you to marry so that for once you could focus on someone else but yourself. No, I didn't agree with his approach to force you into marriage, but he was desperate. He thought if you could go away for awhile, back to your homeland, you'd temporarily forget about Langworthy Lumber. But nothing could get through to you, not even his death."

Thorn stared at her. "You, like Sandy, think I drove my father to the grave!"

Veronica had said enough and regained her composure. "Go get her, Thorn. She's your last hope. I just feel it in my bones. God brought his woman to you. Why are you letting her slip through your fingers?"

He didn't reply and she rushed on, "For goodness' sake, she's traveled all day on little food and looks exhausted. All this commotion over a silly telegram!"

Thorn straightened his tie, glancing at Veronica before striding out the front door. He noticed the servants ogling at the windows. "Back to work, every one of you!" he called over his shoulder. They scattered like birds, but after the front door slammed, they rushed back to the windows. Thorn walked to the stables where the stable boys, not missing a cue, had a trap ready for him.

Sandy passed him in the drive saying, "She won't come back. I tried to coax her but she'll have none of it."

Thorn didn't reply but snapped the horse into a light trot.

Sandy joined Veronica and Lewis at the window. Together they watched Thorn Langworthy do something he had never done before: pay for his actions. At length, Veronica said quietly, "She's the one."

Phyllida's feet ached from the delicate heels. Undoubtedly she was tired, but her anger fueled her along. What was she thinking? How could she be so foolish as to leave the school, all of her students, and her dear friends? She nearly laughed. She could hear Ada saying, "Slow down, my dear. You're too angry to set your thoughts right. Give it over to the Lord."

Phyllida heard the sound of a trap rolling up behind her. She quickened her steps.

"Hello."

She knew the voice but wouldn't turn around.

"You're not speaking to me?" Thorn asked in attempt to be charming.

She squared her shoulders and continued forward, uninterested.

"I want to talk to you," he said.

Phyllida ignored him and continued walking, her eyes straight ahead, her lips pursed in determination.

The trap stopped and she heard him leap off. He jogged up beside her and lightly grasped her arm. She flinched and recoiled, glaring into the dark eyes of Thorn Langworthy.

For a moment they watched one another, each sizing up their opponent and measuring their defenses. Had he not been so uncouth, she would have considered him very handsome. Thorn Langworthy towered over her and exuded a kind of masculine power she would have found appealing, had he a personality that matched the fine chiseled face and unusual eyes.

"I suppose I deserve your anger," he said flatly. Where would be begin to fumble through an apology? He was unused to such a custom.

"You 'suppose' right." She began to move on. He followed her as his horse followed him. With dismay he realized they were nearing town. Thorn knew this would create a buzz.

"Will you stop so we can talk?"

She set down her case, crossed her arms and looked down at her dusty, unpractical heels. "Go on."

She was not going to make this easy.

"I don't think my behavior was…appropriate. Perhaps I was a little too angry that you didn't telegram me in New York."

"I agree— " she began

"I'm glad you understand my frustration— "

"I was going to say that I agree your behavior was very inappropriate." She was being tough on him. How long would his patience last? He glanced at her small frame, her slender arms crossed across her chest while her pointed shoe tapped impatiently. Her eyes glared into the woods while her mouth was pursed in what he thought was an adorable pout. He didn't remember the last time he had thought of the word "adorable" when looking at anything, or anyone.

"Well, do you forgive me or not?" he barked.

She turned. "When you put it like that, I have to graciously decline."

He really disliked sarcasm.

She strolled forward and he cleared his throat. "Miss Cowen, wait."

She set down her case again. "Yes?"

"I'm…sorry."

"For what exactly?"

"For…being so terribly rude to you…and for…shouting at you."

Her face softened as she mulled over his words. The pause lasted uncomfortably long and Thorn shifted, kicking at a rock. Why did he suddenly feel like an adolescent boy?

"You're forgiven, but I can't possibly accept employment at Twin Pines." Why had she said that? Where did Phyllida have to go? She had little money and no prospects. But something within her wanted to make him beg her to stay.

"I will be easier to work for, I promise."

"How can I know for sure?"

"I give my word," he said, "to be as...flexible and as generous as I can be. You seem to be a very intelligent, kind lady. We would like to have you stay... very much."

She hesitated and glanced around. She chewed her bottom lip as if contemplating. "I will stay," she raised her finger, "temporarily."

Thorn wanted to bark, "What do you mean, temporarily? Have you a better offer?" But he knew otherwise.

He nodded in agreement and took her case to the trap. Neither spoke until he helped her step up into her seat. Her next words struck him. "In what capacity will I serve? I'd like to begin right away."

"I thought perhaps...as a companion." Why didn't he have his reply better planned?

"To whom?"

"To me."

Phyllida turned to stare at her new employer. "I beg your pardon, Mr. Langworthy, but I hardly consider you in need of a companion."

"What I need is a secretary," he rushed on. "I need someone to correspond with my associates and investors, arrange meetings, dinner parties, help me to host and entertain potential customers..." He usually had his efficient secretary, Mr. James, do this, but what was he going to say to the hothead: "Now that I've hollered at you, will you marry me?" No, he would have to be a bit more subtle.

"What makes you think I'm capable?" she asked warily. She couldn't imagine working at his side, even in her most poised and patient moments.

"I have an instinct," he said quite frankly. She seemed honest, intelligent and a little shy—not to mention with a temper. He glanced at her mouth again but not without her seeing him. She turned away hastily. *She doesn't like me*, he thought. Yet he had four months to get her to marry him.

As they headed home, he talked lightly of his business. He had to curb himself from rambling on about his foremost passion. Thorn wanted her to see the vast beauty of logging, the way the lumber smelled, the pleasing sound of an ax splitting a great, majestic tree. He loved the way the tree rushed to the ground with a blast of air. But his greatest pleasure was seeing the crème boards rolling out of the mill ready to be molded into one man's dream, or another man's necessity.

He realized he had been talking of such things for several minutes. She was listening, he could tell. He was a great observer of gesture and by her quick eye movement; he sensed she was internalizing all he had to say. "Do you have plans for expansion?" she intelligently asked.

"Yes, I plan to purchase several thousand acres in the Upper Peninsula."

"Then why the hesitation?"

"I have larger issues at hand," he said, amazed that she was so quick on the draw.

"Such as?"

"The 'jacks are disputing."

"Jacks?"

"The lumberjacks," he corrected himself. "There have been several fights and a few petty crimes."

"Due to low wages, poor living conditions, or both?"

He turned. "What makes you suggest so?"

"About fifteen miles south of Grayling, the train went through a lumber camp. It was near lunchtime and I saw the mess tent. It was plain to see that whatever they were eating, it was runny and sparse. They ate from small bowls and drank from little cups. Their tents were another sight: small, dirty, and in need of repair. I noticed several men coughing and looking rather malnourished. At first I thought it was a prison camp. But my traveling companions said something about Langworthy land."

"That's camp six, near Roscommon," he said. "I didn't realize…"

"Have you toured the sites? I saw only this one and it was quite unfavorable. The men were unusually thin and gaunt. These are the men who cut down such great pines? I'm surprised there haven't been any fatal accidents." Phyllida knew she was speaking her mind, but she had compassion for their working conditions.

Thorn didn't like what she said either, but he mulled over her words. "You will accompany me on my tour of the sites, starting tomorrow. I want you to look at things with a critical eye and tell me ways I can improve the situation."

"Am I correct about low wages?"

She was smart, he thought.

"I did decrease their pay, slightly, but not enough to cause that much trouble."

"I guessed so because I overheard a couple of men at the train station discussing 'missing pennies' from their pay."

Thorn knew people in town would talk about it. Any news was huge news in Lovells.

"Did you overhear anything else of interest?"

She thought she had heard someone refer to her as "Thorn's bride," but certainly she misunderstood.

"No, nothing worth mentioning."

Dinner was a strange affair, she thought.

Sandy and Thorn were waiting for her as she entered the dining room. She took care to dress in a pale yellow gown, very simple and, as Thorn noted, very outdated. The dress fit her petite frame with a slight bustle that gathered the layers of petticoats from behind. Thorn had thought her hair was somewhat attractive; it was a heavy, rich gold color with unruly, fine locks that escaped around her face and neck. Phyllida Cowen was small, but beneath her large, bewildered brown eyes lurked a stubborn streak. Her nose, what the French would call pert, and her full lips gave her a sort of Mediterranean look. She spoke English, and exuded English customs, but her face seemed less than English. She did not posses the frail, white skin and blue eyes so common among British. She had indicated that her father, like Thorn's, had been

Cornish. The Cornish were dark in features with olive skin. It didn't matter. Her birthright was British and that's all he cared about.

Sandy and Thorn stood by their chairs as Phyllida began to sit. Then, realizing her folly, she immediately stood. "I'm sorry…"

"It's all right, Miss Cowen," Sandy said lightheartedly. "Thorn likes us to have a formal word of prayer before dinner."

They bowed as Thorn lamely mumbled excerpts from the Lord's Prayer. She thought the prayer sounded stiff rather than heartfelt. When they murmured "amen," she waited hesitantly. The men, waiting for her to sit, looked on.

"What custom takes place next?" she asked, slightly exasperated.

"We're waiting for the lady to sit," Thorn said, his own patience slightly ebbing.

She wanted to retort, "You must inform me of these 'customs' if you want me to adapt without inconveniencing," but her own reservations kept her silent.

Thorn, after he tried the soup, asked, "Where's Lewis this time?"

"I suppose he's running a bit behind," Sandy replied.

"I know he's running behind; where is he?"

Lewis entered, his eyes trained on Phyllida. He was a shorter, younger version of Thorn with the exception of the dimpled smile he flashed. "Hello, sorry I'm late. I'm glad you've decided to come back, Miss Cowen."

"You're late," Thorn said flatly. "You know I don't like tardiness." He wasn't sure what annoyed him more, Lewis's tardiness, or his fawning over Phyllida.

"Forgive me, Brother. I've been with Hamilton down at camp seven. Seems there's been another fight. This time it took out the cook and two of his assistants." Thorn put down his soupspoon and called to the young girl hovering nearby, "Annie, this soup is cold. Must I always send back my food whenever I sit down to eat?"

"No sir." She hurried away.

"What was the scuffle over this time?" Thorn asked, turning his attention back to his brother.

"Apparently the cut in the men's pay has caused a to-do, especially considering the food has not improved like you had promised."

Thorn did not speak. Sandy looked annoyed.

Why does Thorn's presence cause such anxiety? Phyllida thought.

"Miss Cowen and I will look into matters tomorrow."

Lewis nearly laughed. "You're not serious!" he said, glancing at Phyllida.

Thorn shot him a stony look and Lewis humbly turned to his meal, but now without suppressing a smile.

After dinner, Thorn had walked her to the staircase, his brothers looking on quite curiously. He bid her good night, asking her to meet him promptly at seven o'clock the next morning.

Phyllida was glad to be in the quiet of her room and wasted no time sinking into bed. She sighed. *What kind of people are they*, she thought? Lewis and Sandy, like everyone else, were obviously intimidated by their brother. Was that any way to live? Perhaps Thorn held the purse strings for both brothers, and they were dependent on him for their livelihood. It seemed the servants skittered about nervously. She didn't blame any of them either. He was quick to shout and eager to argue, she thought. Why did he want her help? Certainly he seemed capable and sure of himself, and her assistance wasn't necessary. Judging by the coach class ticket, he wasn't exactly generous either. Why had he really paid her uncle's debts? There was a motive and she was going to get to the heart of it.

The morning went surprisingly well.

Thorn and Phyllida met in the dining room. They exchanged curt greetings and turned their attention to the breakfast Edith brought. Phyllida had never had such a fine meal, especially for breakfast. Scrambled eggs, buttered toast, sausage patties with thick gravy and fresh marmalade made her mouth water. However, she was unaccustomed to eating in the presence of a man. Remembering Ada's advice of "dining delicately, eating politely," she ate a slice of toast and sipped hot coffee.

They made their way to his office, which was located on a barren strip of land. She smelled the scent of fresh lumber and noted the ravaged pine stumps and small ravines where the dynamite was used. He explained the purpose of the myriad of paperwork as he showed her around the small office. The crude log building held three desks, several mounds of paper and a smaller table where it appeared the men ate.

"About sixty miles north of Grayling," he answered. Handing her a pencil and tablet, he said, "Take notes of what you see and how improvements could be made." She nodded and he led her out to the trap where they began their tour of the land. Thorn motioned to the trails throughout the woods. "These are logging trails. When the wood is cut, the jacks must take them to one of two places for transportation: the river or the railway. Unfortunately, the railway is more expensive, but that is our best alternative until there is snow and ice."

The trap bumped through the uneven logging rail until they reached a large railway where men were using a sort of crane to pick up massive logs and stack them on the flatbed cars. She couldn't help but notice the lumberjacks looked tired, as well as unusually thin and gaunt. She noted this in her book and they moved on.

"Why don't you solely use the river for transportation?"

"As I mentioned, the weather has to be cold and snowy to easily slide thousand of logs into the river and move them south into the Great Lakes. Let me show you." They moved on down another logging trail and soon came into a clearing where they were greeted with the rush of a gurgling river. As they moved along, Phyllida was struck by an interesting sight.

The river was full of logs, so full that the river all but disappeared. Within this sort of log jam, young boys stood on logs, hopping and running backwards to spin the log while using a sharp stick, called a cant hook, to poke a log that hung up on the shore—all the while moving slowly downstream. They boys played cheerfully while singing a quirky song about fair maidens and death to lumberjacks.

"In the winter," Thorn explained, "the riverbank is icy, thus making it easier to slide the logs into the river. The current is so strong that it's sometimes easier and faster to send them south to the mills waiting for them in Bay City. For now, while it is warm, I use the river to send smaller loads. Come winter, all logs will be transported this way, primarily because it saves money."

"I heard Sandy mention something about a log branding. Do you brand your logs as one would brand livestock?"

He nodded. "Believe it or not, if we're not careful and watchful, these massive logs could be stolen. There are rings of log thieves everywhere who make a fortune on stolen wood. Therefore, the logs are branded with the Langworthy crest in hopes that mill owners will see that the logs are stolen. Sometimes that doesn't always work."

She observed the young boys, who waved at her. She waved back. "Why are young boys allowed to do this if there's the possibility of thieves about?"

"This sort of log transportation needs small, thin men—or in this case, boys—to do the job. If an average man did this, there would be a greater chance he could fall in and slip down between the logs. The current would be too strong and the logs too heavy for him to work his way out. And most usually, he would drown"

She shivered. "How awful."

At length, they headed to the closest camp, camp seven. The jacks, as Thorn referred to them, were cutting away, smothering trees. She noted that even smaller, immature pines were cut. She made note of this to Thorn, who said, "All trees must go."

"But they're not fully grown!"

"We wipe out one area, pack up and move on to the next, never to return to the former site. We cannot wait for trees to mature, and then come back for them."

The campsites were as she expected. The men looked starved and thin. She browsed around the empty mess tent, glancing at the breakfast dishes. A cook was scraping the last of the watery, gray gruel into a pan. When he saw her appalled glance, he murmured, "It's all I got to work with, Miss." She nodded.

The tents were made of a thin canvas material that was cheaply made and poorly sewn. She was no seamstress but the stitches were obviously pulling out. The tents were faded from the sun, and some had holes. She glanced into one tent and saw where a rusty can collected water through a hole in the tent. Thorn said very little, instead letting Phyllida roam around. The men were off site so she took liberty to inspect, writing down information. At one point, she licked the pencil tip and began to write as Thorn asked, "You must find this place distasteful." Did she detect a little shame? She didn't reply and asked to move on to the next site.

Camp sixteen was in the worst shape yet. The cooks were preparing a lunch that consisted of stale bread, watery soup and slices of runny pie. The men were lining up for lunch when Thorn wandered through the mess hall. The jacks removed their hats out of respect for Phyllida.

She was unprepared for the outburst.

A young man with flushed cheeks and dirty hair stepped forward. "Look! It's Thorn Langworthy with his betrothed. Are you giving the little miss a tour of the dump?" The jacks stirred a bit uncomfortably.

"What's your name?" Thorn asked icily.

"I'm Davis Cleary and this is my brother Frank," he said proudly. Frank, who was seeming to make an effort to mind his meal, turned with a look of dread.

"I don't like your tone, Cleary."

"And I don't like the way me and my brother live like pigs. We're fed week-old soup and sleep in paper tents. Then you show up in your fancy duds with your fancy lady to mock us."

"Hush, Davis!" Frank hissed.

"No one's mocking you," Phyllida said softly. "We're here to improve— "

"That will be enough, Phyllida," Thorn said.

"I think we should explain why we're here— " She turned towards him, her face flushing.

"I don't take orders from females. Remember your place!" he hissed icily.

She didn't reply and Davis Cleary said, "Do you hear that? 'Remember your place.' Those are golden words coming from a man who has to marry to get his pa's business— "

Thorn grabbed the young man's collar and punched him square into the jaw. Clearly fell to the ground, but leaped back onto his feet. "You'll regret that!" he whispered. He lunged at Thorn, but Thorn dodged his advance and tripped Davis, but not without pulling his arm across his back, sending him into the wet earth face first. Davis flipped to his back and pulled himself to his feet. He watched Thorn, as if deliberating whether to continue. Thorn was greater in stature, but Davis was fueled by anger. He threw a punch, but Thorn caught his fist in his bare hand. Thorn's immense hand seem to crush Davis's fist. Davis cried out as Thorn drew his leg towards Davis's chest and kneed him in the stomach, sending Davis down to the ground again. This time he didn't attempt a comeback, and instead watched Thorn with slight fear.

"Get your things and leave my property. I don't expect to see you again—not now, not ever."

"We want our pay for the work we've done so far," Davis said, his face covered in mud.

"You should have thought of that before you opened your mouth to speak."

"You'll regret this, Langworthy. A Cleary never forgets his enemies," he whispered, his chest heaving.

"Neither do I," Thorn said deliberately as he rubbed his knuckle with his hand.

The young man pulled himself to his feet and his brother had no choice but to follow. For a moment Frank glanced apologetically at Phyllida before heading in the direction of the tents. Thorn turned to the rest of the men and said, "Let that be a lesson to you! If I hear of one more fight, or anyone complaining about food and board, you will be fired without remaining pay. Remember, men: you're paid once a month. That's a lot of money to lose for being foolish."

Phyllida was trembling. The confrontation had left her nauseated and weak. She had never witnessed a fight, and was even more surprised at Thorn's unrelenting strength. She also wondered if Davis' comment about Thorn's impending marriage was true.

Thorn knew what she was thinking. She looked white, he thought. She gnawed on her bottom lip, her hands trembling as she began to step into the trap. Phyllida stumbled and fell against Thorn. He gently grasped her arm to help her straighten. She was powerfully aware of their closeness, as she faintly smelled the scent of his soap. He waited a moment before he let go of her arm. He too was a bit startled by the encounter as he looked down at her white face and the thick hair coming loose behind the ears. He wasn't accustomed to caring whether or not people liked him, but he wanted Phyllida to like him. And he wasn't too sure if it was about the inheritance or just because he wanted her approval. Either way, he would have to explain Cleary's outburst.

When they settled in and made for Irving Hamilton's camp, he said, "I suppose you're wondering about that bloke's comment."

She turned expectantly. For a moment he noted the way the slow, pink flush crept back into her cheeks. *She probably knows*, he thought, *why I brought her to America*. He wasn't good at facing consequences, but here goes, "I'm sure you're wondering— "

She asked directly, "Are you betrothed?"

He hesitated, then said at length, "I hope to be."

She smiled lightly. "I must say, I was a little confused by my position here."

"What do you mean? Did you think you were to be my bride?" he asked carefully.

"Well, I noticed how large my room was, the nice eucalyptus...it seemed overwhelming for just a paid employee." Her face was crimson.

"But I don't think of you as an employee," he began.

"...or a mail order bride as it seems. What a relief!" She laughed, then rushed on. "Forgive me, Mr. Langworthy. I've had few life experiences. I suppose I was concerned about the details of the appointed post."

She didn't ask further questions and Thorn nearly breathed a sigh of relief. Phyllida had her answer and it seemed to clear up her previous suspicions. Why then, did she also feel slightly disappointed by his probable engagement?

Chapter 3

A man with red hair brushed off the sawdust and removed his hat as he approached Thorn and Phyllida. Based on Thorn's description, she guessed the slim fellow with green eyes and a wide smile to be Irving Hamilton. Thorn introduced Phyllida and Irving. So glad to meet you," he said lightly. He was the first person she had met so far who didn't seem nervous and unruffled by Thorn's presence.

"Mr. Langworthy, I have the lumber count for you."

"Bring it by later."

"I won't be around. I'm leaving early today."

Thorn frowned. "I wasn't aware of this."

"I had cleared it with Sandy."

"That doesn't matter, you should notify me with schedule changes."

"Sandy's in charge of the foremen, isn't he?"

Thorn avoided the question. "Why are you leaving early?"

"The church is having a small revival. I'd like to invite you and Miss Cowen. It starts at five, and then afterwards we're having a small potluck dinner, hosted by Ruby Dexter."

"I don't eat that late— " Thorn began.

"I would like to attend," Phyllida said. "I haven't been to church since leaving England. Perhaps I could borrow the trap..." She glanced up at Thorn.

Irving didn't miss a beat. "Why couldn't Mr. Langworthy bring you? I would ask Sandy, but he's coming early to help set up for the service."

They waited as Thorn grumbled, "Hamilton, I don't have the time for such nonsense."

"You used to make all kinds of time, Mr. Langworthy," Irving said. Phyllida wondered if he had always called him "Mr. Langworthy," as she sensed a previous friendship had existed between the men.

"I'll bring Phyllida by," Thorn reluctantly consented. "Now let's talk about something of real significance. We need to clean up the head knocking around here. I made an example out of those troublemakers, Davis and Frank Cleary. I fired them and explained to the rest of the camp that I won't tolerate tomfoolery. You make sure the word is spread and enforced."

"Frank's pretty levelheaded. What did he do?"

Thorn couldn't answer and Irving went on, "You assumed he was guilty by association? That's not fair, Mr. Langworthy."

"I didn't ask for your opinion."

They had made their way to the trap where had Phyllida sat down. Thorn and Irving crossed their arms as if ready for battle. "The answer wasn't in firing Davis and Frank Clearly. He's a hothead, but he's frustrated. They're all frustrated." He nodded behind him where the men were finishing lunch in the small, overcrowded tent. "These men are living like they're sentenced criminals. The work hours have increased with even less compensation. The food is bad, Mr. Langworthy. Jake Clawson's lumber company in Bay City serves three excellent meals a day. They work the same long hours, but at least the lodging is more presentable and more of an incentive for them to work."

"Times are tough; they should be grateful for what they get."

"But you're taking advantage of this difficult time. You're getting richer off their malnourished bodies. Please consider some alterations," he said with diplomacy.

"Out of the question," Thorn said. "I've trimmed corners, slimmed down the menu, and as a result, the profits have made Langworthy Lumber the best in the Midwest. I don't even have the benefit of transporting lumber to the bay like Clawson, the lumber tycoon in Bay City. My lumber transportation requires more men and more money, yet we are still leading the race."

"The business shouldn't be thought of as a race, Mr. Langworthy," Irving said.

"But it is," he said. "To lose profit is to lose altogether."

"I don't understand what happened to you, Thorn. Your father was just as ambitious, but I never saw him get this cut-throat."

"Leave my father out of this, Hamilton."

"He wouldn't like the way you're dealing these men."

"I said leave my father out of this." Thorn glared.

"Look at what you've become," Irving persisted, his eyes wide. "You're missing out on life."

"I don't need you to preach— "

"Who's preaching? I'm merely expending a little common sense."

"Is that what you call it? I think you're as odd as the day is long. Remember who signs your cheque so keep your ideas to yourself." He alighted the trap and Phyllida noticed Irving's pinched expression.

Once the trap had pulled away, Phyllida blurted out, "How could you speak to him like that?"

"You know nothing of the matter, so don't start."

Her heart pounded as she built up the nerve to speak. "You were very rude to him. It seems Irving works hard and receives little credit. His ideas were good and his judgment fair. Listen to him. He wants to help the men while keeping the peace," she said lightly, her soft brown eyes pleaded.

"You talk too much," he said.

"You think anyone who has ideas opposite of yours talks too much."

Thorn didn't reply. Why was it every time Phyllida spoke, he found himself listening to her? Perhaps she had a habit of seeing beneath the surface.

Not only was Phyllida surprised when Thorn agreed to attend the revival with her, but his brothers also glanced at each other in complete amazement as he announced that he was going. When Phyllida left to get her bonnet, Lewis leaned forward to speak to his brother. "You're really trying to win her over, aren't you?"

"Hush, Lewis. You prattle like a child. Maybe I want to attend the revival."

"We know you better than that," Sandy said quietly as he prepared to leave. "I'll see you there, Brother."

Thorn's heart sank. Did his brothers really think so little of him? They knew Thorn only made decisions based on self-fulfilling motives. Yet he couldn't blame them for their thoughts.

Veronica smiled, "Just keep it sincere, Thorn."

"I am sincere," he protested.

"Sincere about what? About attending church? Or about sealing a deal tonight? Don't look at me like that, Thorn. I know you too well."

Phyllida met him in the hall. He briefly noted her light green dress with a white collar. Her hair was pulled into a thick braid that was wound in a simple yet pretty bun at the nape of her neck. Her olive skin flushed when she glanced at Thorn. She smiled lightly. "I hope you weren't waiting long," she said.

He said that he hadn't been. As they were leaving, Lewis asked Veronica, "Do you think she'll marry him?"

She shrugged. "I wouldn't blame her if she didn't. Besides, I don't think she has the faintest idea why she's here. Thorn's been having her assist as some kind of secretary. It's really become the talk of town…a female secretary to Thorn Langworthy."

Lewis nodded. "I wonder if she's caught wind of what a to-do her presence has caused?"

"Well, she'll most likely find out tonight."

"Why?"

"There's a potluck dinner after the revival meeting at Ruby Dexter's restaurant."

"Ruby Dexter?" Lewis laughed. "You should have warned Thorn."

"He can duke this out for himself," Veronica said. "I love him like my own boy, but he has a lot to learn and I can't keep nagging him. Some things he'll just have to find out the hard way."

"Poor Phyllida. You're right, she'll figure something is going on once she meets Ruby."

The small church was packed, with folks lining the aisles and walls; men stood and women sat, some fanning themselves while others balanced wiggling children on their knees. When Phyllida and Thorn entered, a silence fell over the humble sanctuary. The pine tongue and groove building created warmth despite the momentary chill in the air. She glanced around nervously. Irving stood and walked towards her smiling warmly. "Welcome, Miss Cowen. Please have my seat." Thorn and Irving shook hands, the previous argument seemingly forgotten. Thorn found a place to stand near Phyllida's pew. She noticed the way eyes wandered between Thorn and herself.

Thorn, too, noted the curious eyes and knew they weren't just because of his pretty young companion, but because Thorn Langworthy was in church for the first time in years.

Pastor Linden took the pulpit after various hymns and announcements. He was a thin, little man possessing a deep sincere voice. Thorn was ready to tune him out. He began to think about ways to tailor the budget to increase profit. He glanced at Phyllida, who was obviously enraptured by the sermon. He sighed with disdain. Was she going to be odd like Hamilton and Sandy?

"...Ask yourself what you've done for the Lord..." Pastor Linden's voice piqued his interest.

"When Jesus asked the young man in Luke 18:22 to '...sell all that thou hast, and distribute unto the poor, and thou shalt have treasure in heaven: and come, follow me,' He knew what a real request He was making of the young, rich fellow. Would you leave everything to follow the Lord? If required, would you give it up right now for Christ?" He paused and a thoughtful silence answered him.

"What did the young man do? Verse 24 says he went away 'very sorrowful.' How sorrowful are you when I ask if you would give it all up for Christ?"

This is the part where he asks for money, Thorn thought.

Pastor Linden was saying, "Ask the Lord, 'What can I do for you?' not how much do I have to give or what's the least I can get away with?' The Lord wants all of us, not just a part."

Thorn thought for a moment. At one time he had given a great deal of himself to the Lord. He remembered when such sermons would warm his heart and inspire him to pursue God's will. Thorn remembered how his mother had encouraged and prayed with him and his brothers. She often said, "Never, ever let the Lord out of your life. Never replace him with material things, they're meaningless."

He thought of her sweet face, her sense of urgency and passion as she begged her sons to acknowledge the Lord foremost in their lives. But then everything changed when he took his first pay and made a wise investment; it doubled months later.

Money is like a seed: when it is planted in the right places and left untouched, it flourishes. He loved the miracle of watching his mere pennies mature into thick, green bills. Soon he found ways to make the thick bills accumulate into hundreds, and then into thousands of dollars. His mind reeled when he thought back to the days when he had watched the logbooks increase in digits. At first his father was pleased. "I've brought you into the business at the right time. You're finally able to begin taking care of things," he had said. With that, Langworthy Lumber was given to Thorn, or so he thought.

For years, money became his object of affection. He trimmed the budget, manipulated accounts, and nourished weaknesses in the business. The results were phenomenal. The business doubled in size so he built a larger office, mindful to furnish it with sensible but reasonable desks and chairs. He maintained the carriages and the lumber wagons rather than buying new ones. Oftentimes wagon wheels split and crashed, but he only forced the men to fix them and make them better. The same went for his workers: when employees became ill or injured, they were quickly replaced. He was driven. Thorn dreamed of more money and more land. More, more, more…

Then his father's health had grown worse. Thorn continued to work, ignoring the signs that his father was ill. He talked to his father late into the night about the business. He showed him the account books even when his father lay ill in bed. Thorn realized with a sense of panic that his father was deteriorating quickly. He then pushed Mr. Langworthy further: "You're all right, Father. Let me just take you down to the new office. You must see the desks, they're made from west Michigan cherry wood, we own nearly seven hundred acres north of Muskegon now..."

His father complied and together they went to the office. His father, wrapped in a thick blanket during the summer, coughed and sputtered. Instead of asking him if he wanted to rest, Thorn pushed further. Somewhere in his mind he thought that by showing his father all he had accumulated for the business his father would heal.

Thorn remembered their last conversation.

It had been another day full of inspecting campsites and prime cutting spots. Thorn took his father to the ravine of white pines, a deep valley that was blanketed in magnificent white pines, each pointed to the heavens. A clear blue sky created the picture of perfection. As they passed a small abandoned cottage, Thorn's father lifted his thin, shaking hand. "Stop here."

"What is it?" Thorn asked.

His father pointed at the cottage that was overgrown in shrubbery, with the windows broken and the door falling off the hinges. "I knew the man who lived here."

"Yes, I recall. I was just a boy, but I remember the old man well."

"I went to him and asked to buy the ravine that this cottage overlooks. He didn't want to sell it. He said, 'You can't put a price on this kind of beauty.' But I wanted the land. What lumber tycoon wouldn't? The man was poor. I knew this and continued making offers.

"'One day,' I told him, 'I'll make you an offer you can't refuse.' I returned a month later and found he had died; his son was boarding up the place. I gave the chap half of what I had offered his father. He was just as poor and gladly took what I offered. If only he knew what I had offered his father." He shook his head. "I cheated him."

"Is that why you won't do anything with the place?"

Mr. Langworthy nodded, and Thorn went on, "The man was a fool to deny your money— "

"I was a fool to cheapen that man's paradise," his father interrupted.

Thorn said bitterly, "To think that would have been my home with Clarice. Perhaps we should have the cottage destroyed— "

"I want it renovated and available so one day Lewis and Sandy have somewhere to live."

"They wouldn't live in such a rustic place." Thorn was appalled.

"Lewis and Sandy aren't like you, my boy. They're like the old man who used to live here. They don't care about wealth, power, or possessions."

Thorn wasn't sure where his father was heading with this. In these last months his father had grown strangely philosophical. He changed the topic. "We're going to start taking down the pines here. We'll bring in a nice fortune with this acreage."

"Don't do it," Mr. Langworthy said.

"What?" Thorn turned.

"I said, don't touch this ravine."

"Why not? These are the oldest, most mature pines."

"I don't care what kind of fortune you can make. Don't pillage this site. Do what you will elsewhere, but this cottage and ravine should stay intact."

"I don't understand."

"This forest is one of the few that haven't been ransacked by gypsy moths or lumberjacks. I cheated that man out of his property by selling his son short. This was one man's paradise. It stays as a reminder to me," the said, pausing to look at Thorn, "and to you, what can happen when greed takes over us.

"I've named this place Thorn's Ravine. It's much like you, son. Look at the jagged ravines and the tall proud trees. At the unseen bottom of the ravine, a small river slips through. There is depth in you, Thorn, though the outside seems proud and jagged, don't forget the deep peaceful stream within."

Thorn didn't speak. Mr. Langworthy patted his son's hand. "It's almost time for me to go, my boy."

"Of course, let's head home…" He found this conversation all too perplexing.

"That's not what I mean." Thorn stopped and turned to his once tall and commanding father, now gray and humped with age and sickness. "I'm going to join your mother in heaven, Thorn. But before I go, I want you to do something for me."

"What is it?" He was willing to promise anything.

"I want you to marry."

"Father!"

"Let me explain. I was an unruly young lad. I was miserable and always wanting more. Then I met your mother. She didn't change me over night, but I saw in her a glow of warmth for her Lord. She showed me how to let go of material possessions and love the Lord. Only," he cleared his throat, "I learned too late. I am an old man now and I think I've disappointed your mother more than pleased her. Now I want to do right. Find a woman like your mother, someone who will be patient and has a quiet, loving soul. Stay away from those frivolous, shallow girls with their silly hairstyles and loud giggles. That's never been your forte, Thorn."

"Marriage is no solution…"

"Maybe not, but living this way is no answer either."

"I have everything I could want."

"You have nothing, Thorn. This could all go up in flames tonight and you would have nothing."

"I have my investments— "

His father thumped his chest impatiently. "Look inside. Where's the quiet stream of your soul?"

He took his father home, realizing his efforts to impress him with the flourishing business were all in vain. Thorn couldn't keep his father alive by showing him how much he had earned. Rather, his father was showing Thorn how much he lacked. Weeks later, as his father lay dying, Thorn dismissed his brothers and weeping servants. After the door closed he nearly crumbled, grasping his father's hand. "I'm sorry if I let you down."

Mr. Langworthy's gray eyes lifted in weak surprise. "You have never disappointed me, Thorn. You're my boy." He patted Thorn's dark hair.

"But if I could have done more, made the business bigger..."

"I don't care a whit about Langworthy Lumber," the father paused, speaking with a strained but powerful voice, "and you shouldn't either. Be young, fall in love, have a family."

"But Father..."

"Thorn," he paused, closing his eyes one last time, "find the bird that sings while it is dark."

"I don't understand."

"You will, Thorn. You will," he said as his eyes closed one last time.

"Papa," he said, pleading, but he was gone.

Thorn nearly jumped when Phyllida's voice brought him to the present. "Mr. Thorn, I'd like to attend the potluck for a little while, do you mind?"

He shook his head. "Of course not."

"Are you all right?" Her dark eyes frowned slightly.

"Yes, let's go."

He ushered her outside where they crossed the street to the small restaurant called Ruby's. She was charmed by the red and white checked curtains and rough wood tables and chairs. The restaurant was decorated in the style of a lumber camp with various pictures on the knotty pine walls. A small fire burned in the grate and along the walls long tables displayed pies, sliced hams, and warm rolls with creamy butter. Thorn spotted a business associate and excused himself. While Phyllida made her way to the punch bowl, a tall, thin woman walked towards over.

"Well, who might you be?"

Phyllida looked up at the woman, her blue eyes twinkling in a cheerful face, her cheeks ruddy as if she spent many hours outside during the winter months. "I'm Phyllida Cowen."

The woman grasped her hand, shaking it profusely. Phyllida noticed how dry and cracked the woman's hands were. "Don't mind my dishpan hands. My, you're as small and perfect as a china doll. I've heard a bit about you, Phyllida Cowen. Welcome to my restaurant, I'm Ruby Dexter."

"It's very charming."

Ruby seemed genuinely pleased. "I've worked hard to make it that way, thanks for noticin'. What can I get for ya?"

"I was just pouring some punch…"

"Allow me."

Ruby handed her a glass of punch and ushered her to a table. "Now you wait here." Phyllida glanced around for Thorn but he was too engaged in conversation with a gentleman in a suit. It seemed he never stopped doing business, even after church. Ruby brought her a plate containing a buttered roll, a slice of apple pie with a piece of thick cheese, and a thin carving of ham fried in butter and honey. "I thought you needed some fattin' up, Hun." She winked as Phyllida began to eat.

Normally she would have felt unnerved with a stranger watching her eat and nicknaming her "Hun," but she realized Ruby, and Veronica for that matter, were like many American women, but seemingly more sincere. This woman was bent on making one feel comfortable and at ease; food seemed to be her way of doing so. Her gingham-checked dress and white starched apron looked like a picture out of a Mother Goose fairy tale. She was pretty in a country way with her hair pulled back into a starched cap.

"Did you prepare all of this food yourself?"

Ruby nodded, and this time she flushed with pride. "My ma was the best cook. She used to set up a pie stand at the lumber camps. Men came in from miles just to get her flapjacks and apple pies…"

Phyllida looked confused and Ruby explained, "Flapjacks are another word for pancakes."

"They sound delicious," she said.

"I'll make ya up a batch some time."

As church members slowly trickled in, Ruby waved them to the buffet as a young man brought out more mugs and coffee. Her restaurant was organized, clean and efficient seeming more like a large family gathering than a business. Moments later, the door opened and Ruby, in mid-sentence, turned to holler, "Get a plate and make yourself— " but stopped when she saw Irving Hamilton.

They glanced at each other in embarrassment. Her voice cracked slightly as she finished her sentence, "—you takin' coffee tonight, Irv?"

He nodded and made his way to the buffet.

The sparks between the two did not go unnoticed by Phyllida.

"Do you know Mr. Hamilton?" She asked the obvious question, hoping for an interpretation of the exchanged glances.

"Yeah." She turned her gaze back to Phyllida. "Irv is a nice bloke."

"Do you know him well?" Phyllida gently persisted.

"I used to. He's a good worker, fair with the men…" Her voice trailed off as Irving found a seat with mutual friends.

Ruby changed the subject. "How do you like Michigan?"

"Oh, it's beautiful here, it reminds me a little of northern England."

"Yeah, I heard you were from England."

"Does the accent give me away?" She laughed.

"Naw, we just knew the British bride was comin'."

Phyllida swallowed. "The British bride?"

"Why yeah, yer Thorn's bride, ain't ya?"

Phyllida glanced at Thorn, who was still engaged in conversation. The men looked eager as they scratched notes on a slip of paper.

"No, he's marrying someone else, I believe." She hesitated.

Ruby looked surprised. "But Hun, the word is out that you and Thorn are gettin' married."

"No, no," she laughed nervously, "I'm working for Mr. Langworthy."

Ruby folded her arms across her chest before frowning in mock confusion. "Yer workin' for him? How?"

"I'm his secretary."

She wasn't prepared for the roar of laughter that came from wiry Ruby Dexter. She laughed hard, her frame jerking as she slapped the table. Phyllida glanced nervously at Thorn. This time he looked over and frowned. Ruby dabbed at her eyes as she hugged her sides. "Oh, Hun! That was a funny one!"

"But I'm serious."

Ruby leaned forward, her eyes moist with tears. "I'm sure ya are, my dear. But let me ask ya somethin': did Thorn really send for ya from England to have ya do his paperwork?"

"Why yes," she said, flushing as the truth slowly dawned on her.

"How do ya explain his three secretaries, his six accountants and two lawyers?"

Phyllida frowned. "I don't understand."

"Yer to be his bride, Phyllida. He is going to ask ya to marry him."

"No, he has asked someone else," she countered.

"How can ya be so sure?"

"Well…" He hadn't actually specified his fiancée's name or the date of their wedding.

"Do you realize everything depends on his marriage?"

"Ruby, I'm afraid I find this whole conversation confusing to say the least."

"Then let me explain a little. Everything you see in Lovells—the small café across the street, the church building, the schoolhouse, the mercantile, the doctor's office and even the bridge over the Au Sable river—is owned by him." She nodded over at Thorn who had resumed his conversation.

"He runs the show here. See, I'm one of the few left who has sole ownership of their property, building, and business. I pay rent to no one and no one tells me what to do. So I can call Thorn by his Christian name and not Mr. Thorn or Mr. Langworthy. My living doesn't depend on the likes of him. He owns everything and everyone here."

"No wonder people seem a bit distant, almost intimidated by him."

"Intimidated? More like scared. He can break any one of these people. Why, today I heard that he fired the Cleary boys."

"Yes, I was there."

"Their pa worked for the Langworthys for years, since ole man Langworthy came over from England and bought his first acre of woods. But Thorn fired them and their father has to go too."

"That's not true. Thorn fired the sons, not Mr. Cleary."

"But the father's sick, everyone knows it. He can barely work and his sons have to help him. When Davis was fired, that means his father has to go too. They rely on each other. When one goes, the rest follow. That Cleary boy is mean-spirited, but his pa has a heart of gold, when he's sober."

"What will they do?"

"I reckon they'll head south to Bay City and the big mill there."

"What is Frank like?"

"He's the quiet type, but he seems to be a good bloke, if he'd get away from his brother. His pa ain't up to workin', that's for sure, but it's a pride thing. He keeps hobbling along, his boys help him out and they all support each other."

Phyllida felt sick. Poor Mr. Cleary, working awful hours and eating terrible food, and for what? Only to have his sons fired.

She shook her head, changing the subject. "I'm afraid there's been a misunderstanding about my marriage to Thorn."

Ruby didn't speak at first. Then after a few minutes she said quietly, "I'll be here if ya need a place to stay."

Phyllida looked surprised. What kind of man was Thorn Langworthy after all?

Frank Cleary did as he was told. The tree was cut just enough that it teetered slightly. Davis tightened the knot in the rope and held on. "When you see him leaving, give me the sign."

Frank nodded reluctantly and moved in the direction of Ruby's place. He waited for what seemed eternity. The lights from the restaurant glowed. He could hear the laughter, the silverware tinkling, and the sound of clapping as a fiddle played into the night. He felt lonely watching the happiness going on without him. No one in there thought of him today, the fact that he and his pa had lost their jobs because of his brother. It didn't seem fair, he thought miserably.

He didn't even really hate Thorn Langworthy. The man was a money hungry scoundrel, no doubt, but did he deserve to die?

He closed his eyes for a minute. It felt good to be away from Davis's endless chatter of big stories and larger than life schemes. When he opened his eyes, he saw that Phyllida, the girl who had visited the lumber camp, was with Thorn. No, he thought, this has gone too far. He dashed down the trail running alongside the road. He mustn't be seen. He hastily removed his shoes and sprinted noiselessly towards Davis, who waited with the rope tied around the chopped pine.

"Don't do it!"

"What? What are you doing here?"

"He's not alone. The girl is with him."

"Better yet. Thorn and his bride-to-be are a forgotten memory."

Frank lunged at Davis, but it was too late. The tree, becoming too much for Davis to hold, groaned under its weight.

"Wait! Hold it still!" Frank hissed.

But the tree fell forward.

He heard the woman scream, followed by the crash of the carriage.

Frank and Davis quietly ran into the night. Frank stopped to vomit; he had never hated himself more than he did at that moment.

Thorn had sealed the deal with Lyle Kendricks. When the men shook hands, he said, "I'll have the first shipment of pines sent by the end of the month."

Lyle nodded and reminded him, "This is a gentleman's agreement, you know."

"Is there any other kind?" Thorn asked lightly.

After Lyle left, Thorn shifted his attention to Phyllida, who was talking to Ruby Dexter. He wondered what they were talking about since Phyllida looked nervous and worried. Ruby was known for her direct advice and hearty cooking. He reluctantly admired her business mind. She had turned her mother's small hot pie stand into the best restaurant in Lovells. He hated to admit that since she had more customers than his smaller café across the street. He would have to look at hiring a better manager. "Hello, Ruby. Thank you for the excellent coffee."

She looked up. "Any fool can make coffee. Ya didn't even try my honey-fried ham."

"No one makes coffee like you," he said charmingly.

Ruby didn't miss a beat. "I see right through ya, Thorn. Ya'll were tied up in business and couldn't take a minute to sample some real home cookin'. Do ya always do business after church?"

"I do business anywhere, anytime," Thorn replied. He glanced at Phyllida, who seemed absorbed by her cup of coffee. "Are you ready?"

"Yes," she replied quietly and stood.

"Let's get together some time," Ruby said. "Maybe I'll come by to see you," she said, patting the younger woman's shoulder. "I like yer accent and all; it's fun to hear ya talk all proper."

Phyllida nodded and thanked her for the meal. He saw the way Ruby winked at her with a secretive smile. Something was going on and he was preparing himself for anything. He helped her to alight the trap, and tucked a thick carpet rug around her legs.

"To chase the autumn chill," he said.

"Thank you."

As they drove home the sun was setting, sending the last of its bright red and orange fingers into the horizon. "You're rather withdrawn, Phyllida."

She didn't reply at first. He noted the way her hair curled slightly above her ears. He hadn't noticed the small pearls on her ears before. She looked elegant even though her dress looked plain and worn. She would be a real beauty dazzled in a few diamonds and silk gowns. When she turned away, he gazed at her delicate jaw line and caught the scent of perfume on her hair. He was surprised when she turned abruptly and said, "I know I asked you before, but…are you sure you're intending to be married?"

"Pardon me?" He smiled.

She flushed. "I mean, is it true that you're to be married?"

"Oh yes, it is true that I will marry."

"I see. Does she live here, in this area?"

"Well," he paused, "yes."

She seemed to relax. "I just thought…"

"What did you think?"

"I was told… I mean, I thought…"

He knew where this was leading. *She has to be told*, he thought.

"Well, if you were thinking I was intending to propose— "

Suddenly he heard the slow, steady sound of splitting wood as if a tree was giving way against its weight.

It happened in seconds.

It was almost dusk, and they were surrounded by trees. He couldn't tell which one was falling. For two frightening seconds he glanced around, bringing the horse to a standstill. Phyllida was moving her hand to point upward as her lips pulled back into a grimace. "Thorn! Thorn!"

The tree was hurdling towards them. "Jump, Phyllida!"

"I can't move! My feet..."

Her feet had been wrapped in the blanket and she struggled to release herself.

With Thorn grasping her with all of his might, they jumped out of the trap. He threw Phyllida to the ground and covered her with his own body. He felt the swish of air followed by several branches collapsing on his back. He heard the trap crush beneath the tree as the horse screamed. His heart raced. Neither spoke for a moment as he looked down at her. Her eyes were closed and when she slowly opened them, she said, "Thorn, oh Thorn, I thought I was going to die..." and she began to cry.

He gently touched her face not quite understanding the protective instinct that swept over him. Words stuck in his throat as he struggled to make sense of the whole ordeal.

"Hey, are you all right? I can't believe your horse isn't dead! I doubt he'll be able to be harnessed again, though, look at him! He's jumpy!" Two passers by, Saul Jacobs and his son Bill, who had heard the crash attempted to steady the nervous animal.

"What caused this tree to fall?" Saul shouted to Bill, who was helping Thorn and Phyllida stand.

The boy looked closely at the fallen tree. "Pa, someone chopped at it!"

"It was planned." Thorn saw the rope around the tree where it had been released. "Someone tried to kill me. Bill, will you send for Sandy? He's either at church, or at Ruby's." Then turning to Saul he said, "Help me get Windy out of his harness before he kills himself." Together the men steadied Windy enough for Thorn to quickly unclasp him from his harness. Sensing his freedom, Windy bucked and galloped towards Twin Pines leaving a cloud of dust in his trail.

"He's spooked, but I think he'll be fine, Mr. Langworthy," Saul said. Turning his expression to Phyllida he said, "I think she's needing some help, sir."

Phyllida clutched her shawl, her face white with fear. Thorn placed his arm around her, steadying her. Saul discreetly excused himself to speak to the townsfolk who had heard the commotion.

"I'm sorry, so sorry..." Thorn murmured.

"Who would do something like this?" She was about to cry again.

He brushed away her tears with an unexpected kindness that surprised himself. "I'll get to the bottom of it."

She suddenly felt tired and for the first time in his life, he experienced compassion for a shaken demeanor. How could he make this better? He didn't know how to soothe her. He gently grasped her neck and pulled her towards him, his large hands embracing her small face. She looked up afraid and caught her breath. She didn't trust him. Could he blame her?

He lightly kissed her forehead, something he had never done before, especially without invitation. "Everything will be better tomorrow, Phyllida." He spoke in a tone meant only for her.

When he walked away, her heart ached. She could still feel where his lips had touched her skin. Why did she find herself deeply attracted to an obviously difficult man? There could never be a future for them, she thought miserably.

She sat down while the men stood in groups discussing the event. By this time it was dark and another trap was rolling down the road. When Thorn saw that it was Sandy, he commanded before Sandy could ponder the disaster, "I need you to take Phyllida home right away. Send for Doc Armstrong, and Veronica. She'll know what to do with Phyllida."

Sandy nodded mutely and helped Phyllida alight the trap. She turned and looked longingly at Thorn. He was involved in talking with the men, describing what had happened. As they pulled away, she dropped her head into her hands and breathed deeply.

She didn't see Thorn watching after her.

He didn't know what shook him more: the pine that had hurdled towards his skull or thoughts of Phyllida Cowen. What was happening to him?

Chapter 4

Phyllida could not rest.

She kept a brave face as Veronica and Lewis did their utmost to keep her company. She drank a warm cup of tea and waited for Thorn to return.

"Who would do such a thing?" Veronica shook her head as Lewis paced the floor.

"The Cleary brothers may know something about this," he said. "I heard that Thorn fired Davis and I'm sure he's on a rampage."

"Where's Sandy?"

"He went back to help Thorn," Phyllida answered.

Even though it was a warm autumn evening, Phyllida's body felt cold. She was pleased when Veronica gave her another cup of tea and Lewis burned a modest fire in the grate. They waited for Thorn as the clock chimed cheerfully. Eventually the front door opened and he stood on the threshold, his eyes immediately searching for Phyllida. An older, white-haired gentleman accompanied him. "I met up with Doc Armstrong who was en route to see our young patient," he said, his eyes never leaving Phyllida's face.

"I'm quite well, just a little shaken," Phyllida protested weakly.

"Let me be the judge of that," Doc Armstrong said kindly then nodded to Veronica. "Will you give me a hand?"

The three of them made for the stairs and Phyllida turned to Thorn. "Will I meet you at seven tomorrow?"

"No, I think it's best that you rest. I will look over your notes and begin some work on the camps we toured."

"Do you promise?" she asked.

"I promise," he said reluctantly. Thorn honored all promises, but this was one he didn't agree with. Fixing tents and increasing menus would certainly throw off his polished budget.

Veronica led Phyllida and Doc Armstrong upstairs. Thorn turned to his brother. "Are you thinking what I'm thinking?"

"It was Cleary, wasn't it?"

"No doubt. That tree could have crushed us like ants, Lewis. The sheriff has been summoned, but I've been told that Davis was seen tonight at the tavern with his cronies."

"Alibi or not, he's behind it," Lewis said.

"I agree, but he has friends."

Thorn sat down. He was pale. "What if that tree had killed her?"

Lewis, perplexed by Thorn's comment, replied coolly, "I suppose you'd have to find another bride."

"You fool," he hissed, "I don't care about the marriage issue at present. What if the tree had killed Phyllida?"

"You suddenly have a conscience," Lewis said quietly.

"Forget it." He stood. "You always speak out of turn…"

"Thorn, you expect us to believe you care for her? You 'hire' her as a secretary, dash her off to church and then appear sick at the thought of her nearly being killed? If anyone's a fool it's you. You're pretending and I'm not buying it. She's a good lady, Thorn, and I think she's too good for the likes of you." Thorn didn't reply and Lewis murmured, "If you care a whit for her," he nodded upstairs, "then let her go. She doesn't know what she's in for, though I think she suspects."

"You really dislike me, Lewis, don't you?"

"It's hard to like you, but I'll always love you."

"Don't give me that 'love' rubbish. You've wanted Langworthy Lumber from the beginning. You're jealous of me."

"I'm envious that you are the better looking of all of us. You have the mind power and shrewd business sense to make Langworthy Lumber rise, but I don't envy the shallow, lonely man you've become."

"Get out..." Thorn said wearily.

Lewis made for the door where Doc Armstrong met him.

Thorn quickly asked, "How is she?"

"She's very shaken, and has some scratches and bruises. I've given her a small dose of laudanum."

Thorn thanked him and at length Doc Armstrong commented, "You look a bit white yourself."

"I'll be fine. Thank you for coming out so late," he said, walking the doctor to the door.

"Who's behind tonight's episode?" Doc asked.

"It's hard to say." Thorn didn't want to reveal too much without proper evidence.

"Knowing you, you'll get to the bottom of it," he said. "Just be careful."

"What do you mean?"

"People can be ruthless, especially when driven to desperation."

"Just what are you saying? Are you making excuses for whoever rigged that tree?"

Doc was an old family friend, and a close friend of his father's. He knew by the way the doctor shifted his medical bag as if he were pausing to group his thoughts that he was about to get the brutal truth for the second time that evening.

"You're not doing right by the jacks. They're malnourished. I've treated a couple for diarrhea and several more for head lice."

"Thank you again for coming by, Doc," Thorn dismissed him.

"Don't be stubborn. Your father wouldn't have had it this way."

Thorn, who usually had a reply, said nothing. After he had let the man out, he sighed and leaned against the door. He turned down the lantern and began to make his ascent to his room when Veronica stopped him in the hallway. "Thorn, I'll be letting myself out."

"Veronica, I didn't realize you were still here," he said.

She waved her hand. "No bother. I was in the kitchen explaining to Edith that Phyllida should not be disturbed until tomorrow morning. I took the liberty of ordering her a late breakfast."

"Thank you," he said. "What would I do without you?"

"Manage nicely, I suppose." She laughed as Thorn helped her with her cloak.

"Thorn," she said, and then paused.

"No, don't lecture me," he said, recognizing the tone that was laced with impending reprimand. "It's been a long night."

"It's been terribly long," she agreed. "But, like you, if I don't get my troubling thoughts into the open, then I go mad."

Thorn sighed.

"I think you should send Phyllida home," she said flatly.

"Did she say she wanted to leave?"

Veronica ignored him. "The first time I laid eyes on her, I knew she was a special girl because of the way she stood up to you. She has not been told the truth, Thorn. You're misleading her with your stated intentions of renovating the sordid camp situations. She feels useful here, almost needed. But the minute she finds out what you're really up to, she'll be crushed because she's been made a fool of."

"I'm not making a fool of Phyllida."

"You're patronizing her, making her believe her contributions are most worthy. I think you're pacifying her to manipulate. Tell her the truth soon, Thorn. Tell her tomorrow. I'd take it upon myself to tell her, but it's as I've said to Lewis, there are some lessons you must learn without old Ronnie's help."

Thorn was thoughtful. "I don't want her to leave us."

"That's obvious, as you need the inheritance."

He shook his head. "I don't know if that's completely true."

She looked doubtful.

"Why don't you believe me?" His patience was ebbing. "Why are you all so quick to disbelieve me?"

"Thorn," she said, tying her bonnet, "hidden in your heart are the truths your mother earnestly taught you. But somewhere along the line you've let go of those principles. Certainly you adhere to tradition and are an upright citizen, but you have shoved God so far out of your life that you cannot remember what peace feels like."

She turned to go and Thorn said, "Can I ask you a strange question?"

"I love strange questions because they usually require strange answers. What is it?"

"Before Father died, he said something odd to me: 'Find the bird that sings while it is dark.' Do you know what that means?"

Veronica's face lit up. "I remember your mother saying that. Yes, I do m'dear. But it's an answer that I had to find on my own. If I tell you what it means, you won't appreciate it. You need to experience it for it to make sense."

"I don't like riddles."

"This isn't a riddle. Your father gave you a pearl of wisdom," she glanced upwards, her voice echoing in the hallway, "greater than all of this."

"Why is life so complex?" Thorn mused.

She took her leave. "Think about what I said earlier, m'dear. You must ask yourself, when that tree hurdled towards you tonight, did you think about your financial ledgers? Or did you think about the potential last few seconds of your life?"

Thorn didn't hear the door softly click as Veronica left him alone in the great hall that his father had proudly built.

Phyllida woke feeling achy and groggy. "The soreness is from your body bracing in fear, Miss," Edith said as she drew a hot bath for her.

She glanced at her watch. "It's nearly noon!"

"Miss Veronica thought it best that you sleep," she said, bustling around the room opening drapes.

Phyllida sighed. The sun danced across the lake and a fat white cloud lazily stretched across the sky. She thought it ironic that life should continue on; birds chirping gaily, the occasional splash of a fish jumping for its meal, and the distant sound of dogs barking. She should be dead, she morbidly thought. She shoved the thoughts out of her mind and remarked, "What a lovely day."

"It is, Miss." Edith dropped salts into the steaming water and a sweet rose scent lingered around the room.

Edith helped Phyllida out of bed. "I'm grateful no harm came to you, Miss. Your presence has brought something special to all of us here. Annie and Bella sent you these." She showed her two handkerchiefs with a simple "P" embroidered in one corner.

"They're beautiful! I've never had personalized handkerchiefs before." She looked up. "Thank your girls, Edith."

"I'd be glad to." She smiled, leading her to the waiting bath.

Later that morning, Veronica sent a small bundle of flowers with a card wishing her a quick recovery. Likewise, Sandy and Lewis briefly visited to give her a book on American history. She had mentioned her interest in colonial America and was touched when she unwrapped the book.

But she was unprepared for Thorn's gift.

Two days later, Edith tapped on the door. Phyllida noticed her look of faint disapproval as her daughters followed her carrying large garment boxes.

"What is this?"

Annie was beside herself with excitement. "Mr. Thorn hired Maisy, the town's dressmaker, to produce a new wardrobe for you. He bought you three morning gowns, four silks, a taffeta and even a red velvet!" she cried, delighted.

Bella helped her take the dresses out of the box. They spread them around her, the various colors of red, gold, blue and even pink surrounded her. "Look at this one," Bella cried, holding it to her frame. "Can you imagine how pretty Miss Phyllida will look in this gown? Ma'll do her hair up nice, just like she used to do for Mrs. Langworthy." Phyllida was far from excited and she sensed Edith understood perfectly. Before she could reply to Bella's excitement, one of the servant girls showed in Ruby Dexter.

"Good mornin', Sunshine!" She smiled, bringing Phyllida a plate with a tin top. She leaned over and kissed her cheek. Phyllida was touched and motioned for her to sit.

Edith summoned the girls. "We'll hang these up later. Let Miss Phyllida and Miss Ruby be alone."

After the girls reluctantly left, Phyllida turned to the plate Ruby had set in her lap. She lifted the top. "Flapjacks!"

"Yes ma'am! Them are the best flapjacks you've ever had." From the pocket of her apron she produced a fork and a small container of Michigan maple syrup.

Phyllida had never tasted anything so delightful. "Oh Ruby! You've outdone yourself! I had never realized how wonderful American food was."

As she sampled the pancakes, Ruby motioned to the dresses asking again, "What's all this?"

"Mr. Thorn sent them."

Ruby sighed and shook her head. "I'm guessin' you're not so pleased with his high falutin' presents?"

She shook her head. "I don't need or want a new wardrobe."

"Maybe he thinks you do," Ruby said with her usual directness.

"But I like my wardrobe."

She patted Phyllida's hand. "Then you keep wearing your dresses and pay him no mind."

"This makes me feel like he doesn't like the way I look."

"Does that matter to ya?" she asked, raising her eyebrows.

"No, but…"

"Uh oh. Have you gone and lost yer heart to this man?"

"Of course not!" She flushed.

"Don't get all red-faced, Hun. He's a nice lookin' fella, but he can be a real bugger. As long as ya know what you're in fer…"

Phyllida rushed on, "Oh, but I've already talked to him about his marriage plans, and I don't believe I'm part of them."

Ruby leaned over and patted her hand. "You go ahead and believe that, Hun. When you're ready to meet reality, you come down to the restaurant and I'll introduce ya."

"Ruby! The things you say!" She laughed.

"It's none of my business." Ruby rose to go. "Lunch is on so I best be packin' off. My cooks'll set fire to the place if I'm not there." She leaned down and said more seriously, "Until they catch who did this, ya best stay close to Thorn. He may be a shallow skunk, but he's strong."

"Ruby!" she cried again, laughing at her strange remarks.

"Pay me no heed…" she was saying as she closed the door behind her.

After she had gone, Phyllida paused to finger the watered silk gown that lay across her legs. She rose and put the dress on. The gown molded her shape and though she wore no petticoat, it fell in soft folds around her legs. She looked into the mirror and sighed.

The dress would not do. A deep scoop neck captured the curves of her figure. Her face stained crimson at the thought of wearing it in public. Forever remembering Ada's warning against vanity and her praise of modesty, she turned away and took off the dress. She bathed and dressed in her blue calico print gown. After tying her hair back with a ribbon, she made her way downstairs, wincing from the bruises.

"Mr. Langworthy, the seven dresses and ball gown will be ready in two weeks."

"I would like the dresses ready to deliver in one week," he said flatly.

"I'm afraid that may be too hasty, sir."

"I've spent nearly two hundred and thirty dollars in your store, Maisy. I don't think that is an excessive demand, do you?"

Maisy Owens said lightly, "Of course not, Mr. Langworthy. I shall return the dress we used as a pattern as soon as I am able."

"Thank you," he said as he stepped into the sunlight.

"Thorn Langworthy thinks he can run everything in this town, including my dress shop," Maisy hissed to her assistant, Betty.

"He can do anything he wants considering that owns this building," Betty reiterated. "We'll be working every day and night to get those dresses made for Miss Cowen."

"I wonder why the sudden rush to make the ball gown," Betty pondered.

"I suppose he's arranging a ball to announce their engagement."

"Ruby Dexter says Miss Cowen hasn't the faintest idea. In fact, the girl thinks he's engaged to another."

Betty laughed, "Poor Miss Cowen! She seems like a nice girl. If only she knew..."

A tall pale woman approached the counter. Maisy was startled. "Ah, Miss, I didn't realize you were here. May I be of assistance?"

The woman looked vaguely familiar, Maisy thought. Betty watched curiously as the woman asked, "Did I hear you say Thorn Langworthy is engaged?"

Betty blushed. "I'm afraid you've caught us gossiping, ma'am..." The woman impatiently waved the apologies and asked again. Maisy replied, "That is true, Miss. He's marrying his cousin by marriage, Miss Phyllida Cowen."

"I see," she said, turning to leave.

"Are you an old friend of Mr. Langworthy's?" Maisy was nearly falling over the counter to get a better look at the tall, elegant figure of the woman.

"You could say that," she replied coolly and closed the door firmly.

"Why, what a strange lady! Have you ever seen her before, Maisy?"

"She looks familiar, but I don't reckon..."

The women fell into thick gossip and speculation as Maisy began alterations on a dress to fit a petite, golden-haired girl who didn't quite realize she was about to be engaged.

Thorn talked to Detective Frodell, giving him all the information about Davis Cleary that he could muster. Lewis and Sandy sat stony-faced as he scribbled noiselessly.

"We've checked it out, Mr. Langworthy, and three witnesses said he was with his cronies at the local tavern."

"Check out his brother's alibi. The jacks stick together and will lie to cover each other."

"You can't know for certain," began Sandy.

"He's the most obvious suspect," he said. "He threatened me in front of a group of my workers. What more can you say?"

Detective Frodell scratched his head. "I've checked around a little more and found Cleary's not your only enemy. It seems half your lumberjacks are nearly ready to walk off their jobs. The living conditions are raw to say the least."

"I didn't hire you to inspect the camps, Frodell. Find out more on Cleary. That will be all."

Detective Frodell saw himself out as Edith announced dinner. Sandy asked Thorn, "How is Phyllida?"

"I don't know," he said, preoccupied.

"Didn't you go to see her?" Lewis asked, following his brothers to the dining room.

"I didn't have time," he said, ignoring his nagging guilt.

"It seems strange that you wouldn't go to see her— "

"Sandy, it's been a long day— "

The brothers stood behind their chairs as Phyllida came in apologizing for being late. Thorn's gaze fell over the faded blue gown. Her hair was tied behind her head, leaving thick ringlets cascading down her back.

After Thorn muddled through the Lord's Prayer, he asked Phyllida, "Did you receive the parcels today?"

"I did, thank you." She smiled, he gaze not quite meeting his strange eyes.

"What did you think of the gowns?"

"They're all very pretty," she said, knowing this was going to be an issue.

"Why, then, aren't you wearing one of them?" he asked coolly. Why did she have to be so stubborn? Women loved clothes, didn't they? He pictured her wearing the pink gown, and exalting her appreciation.

"Those were for me?" she asked with a hint of sarcasm.

"Well, they're not for Lewis!" he shouted.

Lewis went crimson. "Say, what's this all about?"

"I gave Phyllida an entire wardrobe as a way of saying, 'Get well soon.' She has shown her appreciation by wearing that old frock." He pointed accusingly at her calico dress.

"Those dresses weren't for me, or intended as a gift. You don't like the way I dress, and thought you'd try to change me. Well, that won't do. The dresses are beautiful, but they're simply not practical."

"Why not?" he thundered.

"They're low cut," she said, flushing.

"What does that mean?"

"It means they're immodest," she went on. "Perhaps I give the wrong impression, but have you ever seen me wear a dress with such a wide...bodice?"

"I don't understand you," he said, frowning.

"That's obvious, Mr. Thorn," she said lightly. "Forgive me for being a bit ungracious. I appreciate what you tried to do, but those large gifts are too much. I would have rather visited with you than be overwhelmed with dresses that aren't suitable."

She was right, he thought. Why didn't he just walk upstairs and pay her a visit? Instead he was thrown into a day's job. Truthfully, he had thought about her, but he didn't think of her. She needed to be shown that he thought of her, especially after nearly loosing her life days before. His self-irritation caused his defenses to flare. "No offense, Phyllida, but I noticed your dresses look like housecoats."

"But they're my dresses and I like the way they look on me," she said with a steely stubbornness that he found annoying.

"That's a fine thanks."

"I'm sorry, but I will not wear those gowns."

"Let me get this straight," he said as he set down his fork. "You choose to.wear that faded housecoat rather than a watered silk gown designed in the latest Parisian fashion?

"That's right."

"You needn't look like a spinsterly school teacher anymore."

"I beg your pardon. I like the self-respect that comes with wearing my wardrobe."

"Have it your way; I'm only sorry you're so ungrateful."

"You didn't buy those dresses for me, but for yourself. Do you actually think I care a whit for larger-than-life gowns compared to a simple vase of flowers, a note of kindness, or a small book? To me those are gestures of generosity and friendship. I was thought of and that, Mr. Thorn, is the sign of a giver motivated by selflessness." She rose quietly. "If you'll excuse me..."

"You're not excused. Sit down." Thorn's eyes were dark with shame mixed with rage.

"I will not be told what to do and what to wear," she said casually as she slid the chair back into place and left the dining room.

Sandy turned to Thorn. "You bought her a wardrobe to ease your own mind, Thorn. She saw right through it and you know it."

Thorn had no reply. Her lack of fear and intimidation angered him, yet he quietly respected her. He glanced at her chair and his heart lurched. He pushed away his meal, no longer wanting his dinner. Never before had he felt so inadequate, and he resented her for the emotions that she stirred within the conscience that had been ignored for so long.

She slowly brushed her hair while gazing into the west. She didn't realize the sun had disappeared moments ago.

Her mind was on other things.

Thorn didn't like the way she dressed and that hurt her pride. Certainly Thorn was stylishly dressed, and had impeccable taste in clothing. She was short and small, so not all fashions fit her well. The dresses he gave indeed suited her small figure, but she did not like the revealing necklines. "There are some things," Ada often chimed, "that are to be left to the imagination." But wearing such a gown would nurture inappropriate thoughts. Perhaps he didn't think of her that way, she mused. Either way, why wear some silly piece of clothing that compromised her beliefs of God's view of a modest woman?

Phyllida turned to her Bible and began to read. Reading God's word was like coming home. Hours slipped by as she found herself reading and re-reading the book of James. She traced her finger along the verse James 1:4 whispering, "Let patience have her perfect work, that ye may be perfect and entire, wanting nothing." She must be patient for God's miraculous and perfect timing. In the secret of her heart, she longed for Thorn Langworthy. *Why?* she wondered. She had never imagined falling in love and here she was falling in love with the most resented and obstinate man in Northern Michigan. Why did she think she could pine for a difficult man and feel a sense of peace? Peace with Thorn would be impossible; peace with God would be most obtainable.

"What will you have me to learn, Lord? Curb the desires of my heart. Let me cease my energy in the wrong directions..." she prayed quietly.

Thorn's dreams unfairly carried him to the same place. This time, the baby cried harder and more loudly. He begged the blurry figure of Clarice, "Let me see my child!" but was answered with shrill laughter.

He woke in a sweat and impatiently threw back the covers. Sleep was impossible once again. He was unable to form his own feelings into thoughts. He dwelled on Phyllida, the scent of her hair, the stubborn tendrils that came loose above her ears. She had looked so disappointed tonight, he thought. She wasn't ungrateful, he acknowledged, just hurt that he found her clothes slightly frumpy and outdated. Thorn paced his father's room. It would always be his father's room. It didn't feel like his, nor did he want it to. The room was full of ghosts of the past as he remembered his mother. He used to wake her with tea while his young brothers would jump on the bed. She never minded but would say to Thorn, "You're always my steady boy." He aimed to please his parents, especially his father. He wasn't given to passions and silly emotions. In fact, he couldn't recall ever being a child. His childhood remembered him as stately, mature though a little temperamental. He didn't laugh at schoolboy jokes or pranks. He was the ever-present ambitious son that his brothers weren't. Why didn't he feel good enough? The room, his parent's room, was a reminder of his quiet, spent youth. Now he was graying slightly. What aged Thorn? Was it his quest for his mother's admiration and his father's approval? Or was it the constant wrestle within himself?

"Find the bird that sings while it is dark…" why had those words never meant anything until now? He stewed while his heart beat with anxiety. He rose and wrapped himself in a housecoat and slid his feet into slippers. The house was quiet as its inhabitants slept. He was making his way to the library when he saw a small flicker of light from beneath the door.

He threw open the door and his heart lurched.

Phyllida, who was looking for a book, startled, and dropped the candle.

They stood in darkness.

The silvery moon filtered across the lake and into the tall windows, throwing the shadow of the windowpanes across the wood floor. He thought she looked haunting with her hair cascading down, her lips void of color and her eyes expressionless.

"You look like a ghost," he murmured.

"You look like you've seen a ghost," she replied.

"They're all around me."

"Pardon?" She frowned.

"Never mind." His eyes were trained on her small face.

She picked up the candle. "I'm sorry I disturbed you."

"I couldn't sleep."

She went to move past him, her eyes downcast. "I wish you a good evening—or what's left of it."

He blocked her way. "Please stay… I mean, if you don't mind."

She glanced at the clock. "It's four in the morning."

"You weren't going to sleep, were you?" he said, glancing at the book about American presidents.

"I… I find sleep impossible tonight and I don't know why," she confessed.

"Come with me," he said, taking the book from her hands.

She followed him but bumped into the sofa. He impulsively grasped her hand. "Just so you won't trip."

"Of course," she consented as her own skin burned from his warm touch.

He led her into the kitchens. He lit a candle, and the grate. An orange glow warmed the expansive kitchen. He led her into a smaller room where a small grate still smoldered flames from the night before. He stimulated the fire as she waited patiently. She glanced at his tousled hair and the way his long fingers worked the match and kindling. He motioned for her to sit and brought her a thick blanket. Soon the little room was glowing with the crackling fire. He showed her to a chair near the fire, and then pulled his chair so close their knees almost touched.

"My father had this room built for Edith. She likes to be near the kitchen, but have a small sitting room of her own. She wanted the coziness of the fire without the draft of the big kitchen."

"Will we wake her?"

"Not if we speak quietly," he said in a low voice.

For a moment their eyes locked and it seemed the last of her shyness left her. She did not feel the need to look away anymore. She bravely met his own gaze as if she answered the questions his own dark eyes held. Neither spoke, as words would break the spell.

At length, they turned back to the fire.

"Tell me about you, Phyllida."

"There's not much to say," she replied, sipping the tea. "My life has been quite listless, but good."

"Tell me about your childhood. Do you remember being a child?"

She frowned. "Indeed. You ask as if you've never been a child."

"I think I was born a man…not a good one either."

Phyllida didn't reply.

"Tell me about you," he said, resuming a gaze that was meant only for her.

She shrugged. "I grew up with my Aunt Chloe and your cousin Ernst. I never knew my parents."

"Did you love your aunt and uncle?"

"Of course," she smiled. remembering. "We were happy. I mean...there were some dark spots… like Uncle's horrible spending habits. But Aunt Chloe always loved him despite his habits. He loved her too, in a way. I had a hard time forgiving him for the years of worry he caused her. Uncle Ernst just couldn't be happy with a simple life."

"I think discontentment runs in the family. My father was the same way."

"How so?"

"No." He smiled. "I want to know more about you. Don't think I don't know your little timid maneuvers."

She smiled softly. "I think after she died, he wanted to make amends for the years of poor financial stewardship. He shifted his affection to me by sending me to school. She always wanted that for me and I think it gave him some satisfaction that I didn't marry off as soon as I turned sixteen. Instead he was able to fund my education." Thorn listened intently as she spoke of her life with her aunt and uncle, then her life at the school. She remembered the happy times with Ada, but she also remembered feeling moments of panic: "Is this all there is?" Her students moved on, most marrying and beginning families of their own. "Somehow I felt left behind. I was happy for my girls," she said, "but at the same time there were pangs of sadness and perhaps envy. Ada and I were left to our, as you say, 'spinsterly' ways. I suppose I was guilty of indulging in self-pity," she said.

"Being alone is difficult," Thorn agreed.

"Indeed. Even with dozens of friends surrounding me there were times when I felt very lonely."

He listened as she relived stories that made them both laugh. He saw in her a vivacious, clever girl who was often held back by her own self-consciousness. "I was terribly shy," she said lightly. "I'm much better than I used to be, but I still cannot keep my face from staining red. Is it not so ironic that I taught voice? Yet, when I sang, I was immediately relieved of panic."

"Why?"

"In my heart I knew that I was doing what I loved best," she said.

He laughed. "Who'd think this little, shy girl before me sings like a lark."

"Singing is a sort of release for me."

"Why don't you sing more often?"

"I would feel foolish. Besides, there haven't been any opportunities."

"Talents aren't meant to make one feel foolish."

"I know." She nodded. "We are our own worst enemy."

"Sing for me now."

She laughed. "Are you serious?"

"I've never been more serious."

"What if I wake Edith and her girls?" She glanced down the hallway where they slept.

"She won't hear you."

Phyllida's face reddened. "I can't."

"Phyllida," he said softly, "nothing in this world would please me more than to hear your lovely voice sing a hymn of the faith."

She breathed deeply. "Do you have a particular song in mind?"

"I like 'Rock of Ages.'"

In the dark sitting room, she cleared her throat and began to gently sing about God's greatness and beauty. Thorn closed his eyes and her voice, exquisitely defined, permeated his heart. He was struck by the sincerity of her tone, and the precise rhythm of expression. She sang sweetly to a God he too used to love. He struggled with wanting to know this God again, but something held him back.

She had finished the final verse when Thorn opened his eyes. "Thank you, Phyllida. So, that's how singing angels sound."

She flushed.

"You seemed to understand the words and meaning behind the song."

"Of course, don't you?" she asked.

"I understand the words, but I don't know if I believe them like I used to."

"I find that very sad," she said.

He sighed. "I am not a good man, Phyllida."

"Yes you are," she said. "But you must find God again."

"I used to know Him. But I don't know what happened along the way…maybe it was greed."

"There's no doubt the Christian walk is littered with obstacles, pitfalls and other setbacks. It's the strong, stubborn Christian who gets up and continues on."

"Have you always been so perfect?" he asked, his expression warm.

Phyllida laughed, then said, "I'm far from perfect, Thorn."

"I don't know what I like more: your laugh, or the way you say my name."

She glanced down at her hands, her heart beating.

"Phyllida, look at me."

She met his warm gaze. "Is there a chance you could care for me?" he asked, leaning over and grasping her hand.

Phyllida looked away. "I certainly care for you, Thorn...."

"But..."

"But...you are not complete."

"What do you mean?"

"Well," she frowned, "how shall I put this? It's like you're not settled. You remind me of a vagabond traveler—it's like you haven't found your home."

He caressed her face, running his finger along her jaw line and along the crease of her mouth. He faintly touched her eyelashes and even the tips of her ears. He thought she was the most beautiful woman he had ever seen, with her thick hair cascading around her small angular face.

"I know what you mean, Phyllida. I can't offer that right now, but I respect you for being honest with me. Now it's time I was honest with you."

Thorn withdrew his hand and sat back as his heart beat fiercely. He began to explain his father's ailing wishes. He explained the significance of the will and the need to marry. She listened intently before saying, "So my presence here is for marital purposes, not because you need a secretary."

"Those were my intentions at first," he admitted. "Then I got to know you. I liked the way you came out of your shell and took a stand against my rudeness. I was angry at first, but had no choice but to respect you for declining the dresses. You've put me in my place, seen me at my worst, and still you don't resent me, do you?"

"I don't resent you," she said. "I must say, I suspected that my presence here was not that of a paid employee. Ruby confirmed this for me but I gave you the benefit of the doubt."

"I want you to believe me now," he said. "I don't want you for the inheritance. I want you for you. I could marry someone else, but that's just it, I don't want anyone else."

"And if I don't marry you in the next two months…?"

"I don't inherit…but that's not the point. I feel I need to be honest with you and I should have been honest with you from the beginning."

"I see," she said, mulling his words over and remembering Ruby Dexter laughing when she told her that she was hired as a secretary to Thorn.

"I feel foolish."

"I know," he said. "It's entirely my fault."

She shrugged. "I suppose only my pride is slightly injured—for the second time tonight. I thought I was really helping you."

"And you are," he said, kissing her hand. "I need you, Phyllida. And to prove it, I will lose everything for you. I want you to marry me when you're ready, not according to my father's will."

After a long pause of gazing into his eyes, she said, "I believe you, I really do."

"Will you wait for me to work things out?"

She smiled. "Always."

Phyllida Cowen was more beautiful than any woman he had ever seen. He wanted to hold her and kiss her just to feel her skin against his cheek. Perhaps by touching her he could redeem himself for all that he had done wrong.

"I don't have any idea what God wants for me."

"Then find out," she said gently.

"I have two months left and I lose everything, and for once, I'm not worried," he said, and then laughed, something he had not done in years. "Isn't it absurd? I never thought I'd lose it all and laugh about it. Do you know why?" Thorn grasped her hand close to his heart. "It's because I have you."

"But God must be met on His terms first, Thorn."

"I know."

"Please pray about this."

"Will He listen?"

"I don't think that's the question." She rose shivering slightly, as the fire had died. "The question is, will you listen to Him?"

She grasped his hand for a moment, letting her hand linger on his shoulder. She turned to go before she succumbed to the temptation of throwing herself into his arms. The time had not yet come.

Chapter 5

Ruby clasped Phyllida's hands. "You really brought Thorn outta of his cave."

"I don't think it's me, Ruby. It's all the Lord's doing," she said after telling her about the evening with Thorn.

"What now?"

She sighed and lifted her shoulders. "I don't know. We could pursue our marriage as we both want…but I think Thorn needs time to dedicate his life to the Lord. I have to keep remembering James 1:4, 'Let patience have her perfect work…' Who would have thought those would be difficult words to live by?"

"Life's ain't easy, but how great it is to have the Lord in our lives. Without him, can ya imagine what kind of life ya'd be leadin' right now?"

Phyllida shivered and shook her head. "I don't even like to think of it, but it keeps me grateful for my eternal salvation."

Phyllida and Ruby sat by the window of her restaurant. Late autumn sent light snowflakes blowing against the window. Phyllida looked outside. "It's bitterly cold out there."

"What's on yer mind now, Hun?"

"I don't like the thought of all the lumberjacks freezing in those little tents with barely warm gruel to nourish their bodies. I don't like it at all."

Ruby leaned back, watching Phyllida chew her lip. "Yer thinkin' about somethin', what is it?"

"I want to help those men," she said bluntly. "If we could do something, provide a warm place and good food, think of those who could come to know the Lord? Picture this," she said, rising. "Located within the vicinity of each camp, we'll build a sort of kitchen, or mess hall where the men will eat three square meals. Dinner will involve a full, three-course meal eaten while hearing the word of God. Then the men will return to their camps, and instead of tents, they will have modest-sized cabins with bunks, warm blankets and a pot-bellied stove."

"Hun, that's a lot of money," she said, but not disliking the idea.

"But it makes sense, Ruby. Without proper food and lodging, how else will they be reached? I've seen how the church attendance lacks, especially for a town of this size."

"How will ya afford it?" Ruby said, bringing her back to their largest problem of financing.

"Well," she gnawed her lip, "perhaps I could enlist the help of the church and the business owners. If Thorn won't fund this, maybe they will."

"Thorn's comin' around to the right way of thinkin'; maybe ya should talk to him one last time before ya find other resources."

She looked uncertain. "I don't think he'll listen to me."

"He will, Hun. Give him a chance."

"Do you think you'd give me a hand if he consents?"

"Sure! What can I do?" she said, her eyes wide.

"I'd like you to hire and train the cooks to prepare meals like the ones here—hearty and filling."

"My ma always said that if ya got a talent, don't hide it. I'd be glad to help." She smiled, seeming genuinely pleased.

As they chatted on, the bell jingled and they both looked up to see Irving Hamilton come through the door.

Ruby's face flushed and she sighed before saying, "What can I get ya, Irv?"

"I'd like a cup of coffee and a slice of that huckleberry pie," he said, gazing at Ruby.

"I can do it, Miss Ruby," one of the cooks called from the kitchen.

"I can handle it, Pete." She winked at Phyllida and rushed off to the kitchen. Irving greeted Phyllida, "May I join you two— "

"Irv, have a seat over here," a group of lumberjacks called.

He turned away reluctantly. One man shoved out a chair with its back to Phyllida and Ruby's table. She noticed that he sat sideways so he could glance from the kitchen to the table where Ruby had sat with Phyllida.

Something's brewing, Phyllida thought with a smile.

Ruby returned with a plate of pie and a cup of black coffee.

"Land sakes, Ruby! Look at the size of that pie! Why didn't I get one that big?"

"'Cuz ya got mush for brains, now hush and finish yer coffee," she snapped in her usual humorous fashion.

The men laughed heartily as the embarrassed lumberjack said, "Aw, you know you love us, Ruby."

"Yeah, like I love a wart!" She turned to rejoin Phyllida.

"Sorry about that, Hun. We're all kinda crude here. I just fight fire with fire."

"I think it's amusing," she said, laughing.

"Now what were we talkin' about— " Ruby began.

"I think there are more important things at hand," Phyllida said, her voice dropping to a whisper. "What is the…situation with you and Irving?"

Ruby glanced at her dry, cracked hands. "Aw, him? Nothin' really. He's a fine good bloke, but… well…aw, it's nothin'."

Phyllida understood her reluctance but delicately persisted, "What is it?"

Ruby rolled her eyes and dropped her voice to a whisper. "We had an understandin' at one time."

"What happened?"

"He got these ideas that he's not good enough for me."

Phyllida glanced over her shoulder and saw that Irving had been watching Ruby again, but turned his attention to his pie.

"It's obvious he still cares for you."

"I still carry a flame for him too. But he thinks because I do pretty good for myself, that it'd be like I was stoopin' to marry him."

"Did you assure him that this wasn't true?"

She raised her eyebrows in exasperation. "I've told him so many times that he's got a good job, and that me and him belong together... I just couldn't get through his thick skull. He eventually called off the engagement and went his own way."

"Well, it looks like he hasn't gone too far. Look at the way he fawns over you, Ruby," she whispered.

"He still won't listen to me. Besides, I got some pride too. I can't be chasin' him around sayin' 'Marry me or get a knuckle sandwich.'" She clenched her fist.

Phyllida laughed and Ruby went on, her eyes warm with sincerity, "It's been two years and I still love him as much as the day I laid eyes on him. But I'm gettin' too old for this tomfoolery."

"There's nothing silly about being in love."

Ruby dabbed her eyes then shooed Phyllida. "Ya best be off, Thorn's probably waitin' for ya."

Phyllida rose and buttoned her cloak. "Thank you for the fine lunch, Ruby."

"Yer welcome anytime. Let me know what Thorn says about your ideas."

Phyllida nodded and stepped outside. Snowflakes skittered around her as she made her way to a small shop at the end of town. She stepped in, gazing at the used furniture, guns and showcases of trinket jewelry. She glanced into her palm and sighed deeply before approaching the storeowner. "What will you give me for these?"

Moments later, she alighted the trap and brushed the tears from her eyes. It hurt to pawn her only jewelry, her beloved pearl earrings. However, she reasoned, it was just material, and the outcome would be long-lasting. As she left the outskirts of town, she passed the place where the tree had nearly crushed them to death. Phyllida turned to see a man emerge from the woods.

He called out, "Hello there."

The man looked familiar. "Frank Cleary?"

He nodded, his face expressionless.

"Why are you on the Langworthy property?"

"I was doing a little hunting."

"Good day to you, Mr. Cleary."

She had started to snap the horse into a trot when he said, "I know what you're thinking."

"That's impossible."

Ignoring her remark, he went on, "You think I tried to kill you and Mr. Thorn."

When she didn't reply, he said, "Well, I didn't do it."

She paused as if contemplating. He had nothing to loose by confronting her, and in fact, could have simply not approached her at all. At length she replied, "I believe you."

He nodded as if grateful. "Don't tell Mr. Thorn you've seen me here."

She thought for a moment before saying, "You should find your way back to town."

He nodded but as he turned to go, he said, "Watch out for Davis. He's really got it in for Mr. Thorn." Then realizing he said too much, he waved good-bye. As quickly as she saw him, he disappeared into the woods.

At dinner, Phyllida listened to the brothers chat about their days. She noticed a difference in conversation as Thorn occasionally laughed at Lewis's mimicry and other jokes. They discussed the winter social over roasted lamb and potatoes. She didn't have an appetite as she gazed at the delicious dinner. It seemed unfair that she should have such an extravagant meal when many went without.

"Does the cat have your tongue?" Thorn asked gently.

"I suppose I'm rather pensive tonight," she said, smiling apologetically.

"Can I have your potatoes?" Lewis asked.

She slid the plate over and at length said to Thorn, "I'd like to talk to you when you have a moment."

He rose. "I'm just finished with dinner. Let's go to the library."

She followed him to the fireplace where Thorn motioned for her to sit.

"I want to do something— "

She was interrupted by Edith bringing in a tray of tea things. "This is Mr. Thorn's favorite desert: raspberry tarts and Earl Gray tea." Edith winked at Phyllida secretively. "There's no better way to a man's heart than through his stomach."

"She is right." Thorn laughed as he bit one of the succulent tarts. When Edith left, Phyllida pulled out a small piece of paper and tried to steady her hand as it trembled. She paused for a moment as the cold wind whipped snow against the window. She thought of the lumberjacks who were probably chilled in their paper tents. She rushed on. "I want something from you that is pricey and you may, in fact, disagree with what I'm asking for."

Thorn's eyebrows raised but his warm expression did not change. "What is it? What has you trembling? Come now, Phyllida, don't be afraid. Tell me what you want."

She unrolled a county map and pointed to various symbols she had drawn. "I want three mess halls built here, here and here," she said as she pointed. "In each mess hall, three cooks and five workers will be on staff to serve three square meals a day. By square meals, I mean substantial quantities that will fill and keep your employees warm."

"Is that all?" he asked with a smile playing around his lips.

"No." She drew a deep breath again. "I also want ten modest-sized cabins built with bunks to house each lumberjack. I know head lice could become an issue, so I figured you could establish hair length regulations. Further, the bunkhouses should have pot-bellied stoves and warm wool blankets. The blankets shouldn't be a problem since the dry goods shop can supply us with at least half now and half by the New Year..."

Thorn crossed his arms in mock concern. "How will this be paid for?"

"I knew you would ask, so I was thinking we could begin by selling the dresses you bought for me. Here is some money." She paused to hand him a neat, small bundle of dollar bills.

"Where did you get this?" His smile faded.

"It doesn't matter— "

"Tell me," he persisted.

"I just got rid of some old jewelry…" her voice trailed then rushed on, "I realize I didn't bring a lot of money of my own into this proposal…"

He grabbed her hands and asked again, "Is that all you want?"

"Lastly, I would like Pastor Linden to preach at the mess hall during dinner. Irving agreed that he would lead service at one camp, and Pastor Linden would work between the two closer camps…" She pointed to the map, but Thorn wasn't looking.

He smiled warmly. "Why are you doing this?"

"Because it should have been done a long time ago," she said, meeting his eyes. "Further, this is an excellent opportunity to lead men to the cause of Christ. Inviting them to church on Sundays doesn't work, we have to go to them, out there," she said, waving at the map.

For the third time, Thorn asked, "Is that all you want?"

"Yes," she sighed, "that's all I want."

He threw his head back and laughed. "Phyllida, my little song bird, when will you marry me?"

She stared for a moment, not understanding the full impact of his question. He rushed on, "I love you. I loved you from the beginning when you stomped out the door in anger. I loved you when I went after you and you stubbornly refused to return unless I apologized. You were tough on me and I loved you for it. I love you for your old dresses, and your little stubborn streak. I love you for your sweet, sweet smile and the way my heart races when you walk in to the room. But most of all, Phyllida Cowen, I love you for loving God and making Him the ruler of your life."

"Thorn," she breathed in emotional surprise. He stood and wrapped his arms around her waist and held her. He kissed her wet cheeks and eyes before kissing her soft mouth. His kiss was gentle, laced with passion she had never known. Her heart nearly burst with love, as she had never experienced such feelings between a man and woman.

"You'll marry me then?"

"Yes," she said. "Yes, I'll marry you."

He held her and at length asked, "Would you like to plan a big wedding for the spring?"

"No, couldn't we use the money for such an affair to put into the lumber camps?"

"That's just like you, Phyllida. Whatever you want."

"Then you'll allow the construction to begin?"

"I'll do more than that." He handed her back the money. "I'll pay for everything including a raise in pay for Irving and Pastor Linden for their willingness to spread the gospel. I'm only ashamed that I let my greed go this far. It took a fallen tree to knock some sense into me."

"Are you saying that you have found God again?"

Thorn nodded. "One evening, when sleep was impossible, I kneeled by my bed. For hours I prayed like this. Soon my deprivation became real to me and I found myself on my face before the omnipotent God asking why he should let me have eternal salvation. It was an amazing experience, one I wish to have as an individual and to share with you. I regret the time I've wasted, Phyllida. Selfishness is like a disease: it utterly consumes and destroys us." He paused, swallowing the lump that had formed in his throat. "I have never known God's grace to be so…beyond my understanding."

Neither spoke and at length Phyllida looked up at Thorn. "When must the marriage take place in order to inherit Langworthy Lumber and Twin Pines?"

"In six weeks, I think, but— "

"Let us marry before then."

"Phyllida, all this is so new to you. Do you want to wait?"

"No, Thorn. I know that I love you and want to be your wife for as long as I live. Think of your inheritance and how we can use that for God's glory."

"Starting with the lumber camp renovations," he said.

"Precisely."

He grasped her hand. "Come, we have a lot of planning to do."

Thorn led her towards his desk and pulled her onto his lap and unrolled a deed to Langworthy Lumber. "If I'm going to inherit this 'dragon,' as Sandy would say, then let's make a few changes…"

Thorn explained the changes as her own heart rejoiced. She quietly thanked the Lord saying, "Thank you for patience's perfect work, for no one else could have made this happen."

After Thorn prayed his thanks for dinner, he bid his brothers and Phyllida to sit. He sensed their surprise that he hadn't muttered through the Lord's prayer, but had actually taken the time to thank God for His rich blessings. He grasped Phyllida's hand and gazed at her as he said, "I'd like to host the winter social this year."

The winter social became a Langworthy tradition in Lovells as the family hosted a large dinner at Christmas time. The Langworthys catered the event with delicious food, including fruits ordered and sent by an ice car from the South. An orchestra, sent from Chicago, played hymns and classical pieces while guests enjoyed singing and fellowship. The social commemorated the birth of Christ, and usually lasted into the late hours of the night.

"What a great idea! We haven't hosted the social in years," Lewis said. "Why the occasion?"

"I would like to announce that Phyllida has agreed to marry me," he said casually, then shouted, "She's going to marry me!"

Lewis and Sandy applauded and shook Thorn's hand.

"She knows why I really brought her here," he said at length. "Yet she forgives me and loves me anyway."

Sandy, who was watching his brother curiously said, "I believe you really love her. It isn't about the inheritance anymore."

"No, not anymore."

"I truly wish you a happy life, Thorn," Sandy said, relieved.

"Brother, I don't think I have ever seen you this…overjoyed," Lewis observed.

"It's not just Phyllida," he said, gazing at her warmly. "It's because the Lord took a mirror and showed me the ugly stains in my heart. I've been in the dark too long and it feels good to be right with Him."

That night, Thorn enjoyed a dreamless sleep.

If Phyllida wasn't planning the winter social, she was continuing to work at Thorn's office. It seemed the weeks were slipping by unnoticed. She and Thorn spent their evenings taking walks or having a small dinner at Ruby's. Their most favorite time was riding horseback through the ravines. She loved the quiet and the great towering pines that shielded them from the cold winds. Though Detective Frodell advised Thorn and Phyllida not to be alone anywhere on the sites, Thorn carried a handgun on his hip while venturing anywhere. Phyllida was rarely out of his sight.

Construction at the sites had begun. Ruby hired the cooks and was in the process of training them when the first mess hall was finished. The mess hall was large with long tables and benches throughout. At the end of the hall an expansive kitchen with deep sinks and wide stoves complete with the latest kerosene lighting made preparing hundreds of meals easier than ever.

The changes at the sites and at Twin Pines seemed to have an effect on the townspeople. Many expressed their gratitude to Thorn who waved them away in embarrassment saying, "The improvements were long in coming." He discontinued his restaurant across the street from Ruby's. "Why bother?" he said. "She has all the local business anyway." Because the building was larger and more centrally located than Doc Armstrong's small office, he leased it rent-free to Doc Armstrong and his patients.

One afternoon, Thorn, Phyllida and Irving toured the last construction site and inspected the bunkhouses. The large cathedral ceilings and knotty pine created spaciousness and warmth. The bunks, roughly made of White pine, framed feather tick mattresses topped with clean linens and blankets. Thorn hired some of the lumberjack's boys to regularly change and clean the linens. It was more than Phyllida had expected and her heart glowed. The mess halls were in operating order; everything falling into place. Irving commented to Thorn, "I never thought I'd see the day, Mr. Langworthy. Because of these changes, you've given more people jobs. You're a new man."

"Indeed, I am," he said, smiling down at Phyllida. "And when are you going to start calling me Thorn?" Whatever tensions had existed between the men fell away and they began to talk like old friends.

On their return to Twin Pines, they passed the office to gather some paperwork. Thorn removed his gloves to warm his hands by the pot-bellied stove. "It's nearly dark, Phyllida. Let's head home."

Phyllida said, "Thorn, I'm very behind in my correspondence letters. Would you mind if I stayed behind?"

"It may not be safe."

"No one knows I'm here. Why don't you and Irving head over to camp twelve and check out the problem with the stove in the mess hall? By then, I'll be finished here and you can pick me up."

"All right," he consented. "We'll be back within the hour."

There was a great deal of filing to do as well as correspondence letters to write. She worked efficiently, not paying attention to the shadow that slipped past the window. The lumberjacks could be heard in the distance shouting "Timber!" followed by the distant thud of a tree meeting its end.

Phyllida hummed softly, shuffling papers and examining Thorn's strong handwriting. She liked the way he signed his name. She found herself appreciating the scent of his soap on the gloves he had left behind.

Suddenly, she smelled smoke. She coughed and reached for the door, only to be burned by the hot doorknob. A fire had been lit outside the door and it was burning quickly. Flames licked past the window, which she frantically opened and shouted, "Help! Please help me!"

Phyllida prayed, "Oh Lord, please keep me calm." She broke a small window with a chair and tried to push herself through, but to her horror, the window was too narrow. With her waist pinched, she shoved herself back inside, feeling the glass bite into her stomach and ribs. The small office filled with smoke and she thrust a handkerchief over her mouth. She paced the room and once again went to the window where she had screamed for help.Then her body grew weak, her lungs burning from inhaling smoke.

Gradually a dark blanket fell over her eyes and the sound of burning timber and the shouts of men became muffled.

The same moment Phyllida was battling for her life, Thorn and Irving were laughing as they relived various episodes from their youth.

At length, Thorn slapped his knee and realized he was barehanded. "We've got to go back. I left my gloves."

"Is that necessary?" Irving asked.

"I'm a creature of habit." He smiled.

"You're actually making light of yourself," Irving said. "I see Phyllida has most certainly inspired you."

Thorn laughed and was about to share what he had read in the Bible that morning when he commented on the pungent odor of smoke. "That's pretty strong. Do you think…" Irving was beginning to ask, but Thorn had already whipped the horse into a wild gallop. As they rounded the bend, he saw smoke billowing between the pines.

"The office is on fire!" Irving shouted.

"Phyllida!" Thorn cried as he leapt off the trap.

"Thorn, wait! The fire's too high. You'll never get out of there alive!"

Thorn kicked the door down, but not without seeing where a board was purposely wedged to hold it shut.

The smoke was rolling in clouds towards him. He squinted and called, "Phyllida! Speak to me!" The familiar lump returned to his throat and he cried again, "Darling! Where are you?" He crawled along the floor, feeling the flames lick along his legs. He spread his hands and felt around the floor, occasionally wincing from the burns. He encountered her limp hand and pulled. The floor started to give way but he refused to move until he had a good grip on her wrist. He pulled her unceremoniously across the floor towards him. He beat the flames that burned her gown, and smothered the fire that burned one side of her collar, ear and hair. He pulled her towards the door where Irving grabbed her and ran from the crumbling floor. Thorn leapt as the boards finally broke and fell into the blaze beneath.

"Is she all right?" Thorn crawled towards her coughing violently.

"She's not breathing!"

"Try! Try to get her to breathe!"

Irving pressed his hands to her face and began to revive her. Painful minutes passed as he continued to work.

"She's not coming out of this, Thorn."

He shoved Irving aside and grasped her limp body. He pressed her close to his chest and planted his mouth firmly on hers and began to inhale and exhale.

"What are you doing?"

"I'm breathing for her," he said between gasps. "Go get Doc Armstrong—now!"

Irving scattered and whipped the horse back into motion. Thorn continued breathing for her and when there was no response, he dropped his head. "If ever you've heard me, hear me now, dear God! Bring Phyllida back to me! I cannot live without her!"

Still the painful seconds continued and at length Thorn thrust his head to heaven and gasped, "Is this your will, God? Do you wish me to love her only to lose her? What is your will? I will do anything, please!" He wept bitterly. Then in a panic, he grasped her limp shoulders and shook her slightly, "Don't leave me, Philly! Come back!"

The blaze continued, demolishing every last timber of the office that represented Langworthy Lumber.

"The burns are not as excessive as they appear," Doc Armstrong was saying.

Thorn wasn't listening. "Why won't she wake?"

"Her body has had a shock. She needs her rest and will eventually awaken," Doc Armstrong said in his usual direct manner.

Thorn felt sick. Sandy, who had been standing by, placed his arm around Thorn. "Even though she's little, she's young and strong. She'll pull through, Thorn. You just have to be patient."

"I cannot be patient during a time like this. Can't I just wake her?" He paced the room like an aggravated lion.

Doc Armstrong's twinkle left his eye and he pressed the agitated man back. "Easy, Thorn. She's not a weakling. Have some faith."

"What if she dies?" he whispered, not hearing Doc's advice. "It will be all my fault, all of it. And just when she agreed to marry me— "

His voice cracked and Lewis, who had been standing with Veronica, turned away respectfully.

"She'll pull through, Thorn. Just wait and pray for her," Veronica said gently.

When Doc left, Thorn sat before the fireplace, his clothes tattered and charred, his hair askew. His smoke-stained hands throbbed where his fingers were burnt. He looked younger, more vulnerable as he leaned his head into his hands and closed his eyes. Veronica motioned for the brothers to leave before turning to Thorn. "Drink some coffee, m'dear."

Thorn shook his head.

Veronica placed her hands on his shoulders and leaned him towards her as he silently wept. She did not speak but allowed him to grieve. "I'm sorry," he was saying, "for everything I've done to hurt those who only loved me." Veronica pressed a handkerchief into his hand and he said, "I can't be any lower than this."

"The tears are good for the soul. You're finally emptying your heavy heart."

Thorn straightened. "I feel responsible for what happened to her—both times."

"I doubt she would want you to be angry with yourself."

"I deserve it, I deserve everything I get."

"It is not just Phyllida that grieves you, is it?" Veronica asked knowingly.

"I didn't do right by my parents or my brothers. I took the respect that I had at one time earned, and dominated them all. Everything was about me, never them, not what they wanted."

Veronica smiled gently. "You're finally coming home, Thorn."

"I don't understand," he said, still refusing to look at her. Crying was the last thing he ever thought he would do in front of anyone.

"Sometimes God brings us to a point where we cannot fathom our circumstances worsening. We see despair, but God in His grace comes from his throne to sit by our side. He's here, Thorn. He's listening."

Veronica let herself out as Thorn hung his head and began to pray.

She floated like a dream. At one point she saw flames and heavy smoke, but they did not disturb her. She wrestled with reality and fantasy as she conversed with gentle voices all around her. Then Phyllida thought she heard Aunt Chloe saying, "He loves you, Phyllida. Isn't love wonderful? No matter what, you'll love him for all that he is and will be." She heard Veronica and Edith chatting lightly. She even thought she heard Lewis reading something about the Civil War. Hadn't he given her a book about the Civil War?

There were moments when her heart beat wildly as her mind, struggling to comprehend reality, saw a man run from the blaze. She remembered hanging out the window, the glass cutting into her flesh. She looked up to see through the smoke a man running into the woods. It was Davis Cleary, or so she thought. She begged, "Please, don't run away. Please help me! I'm burning…"

She struggled to open her eyes, but was pressed back into the pillow as a gentle hand soothed the tears against her cheeks. "You're hallucinating, Darling. No one's going to hurt you." It was Thorn whose voice was ever present. He murmured words asking for forgiveness, and further expressions of his love for Phyllida. Then in the quiet of her own heart, she heard him pray, "Lord, I am most unworthy. Take me instead of her. She's young with a whole life ahead of her. Take me instead."

That was when she opened her eyes and saw Thorn Langworthy. He was bent, his head resting on his folded and burnt hands. He was a great, powerful man exuding every inch of masculinity, broken and beaten as he prayed for his life in exchange for hers. She weakly caressed his arm with her forefinger, and he looked up.

His dark eyes, which she at one time thought looked like bottomless pits, showed the warmth of commitment for Phyllida, and a newly confirmed love for God. She saw the moist tears and the ruffled hair. He looked younger, yet wiser. She saw him through her burning eyes as her own tears irritated the puffed skin.

Words were not spoken.

He grasped her hand and leaned towards her. Just as naturally as one breathes, she gave herself into his arms as he held her gently, his own heart beating wildly.

No matter the trails or heartaches ahead, she knew that her love for Thorn and God's merciful love for them would carry them through.

While Phyllida nibbled at the dinner Edith had brought her, Sandy came to say the sheriff wanted to ask her some questions.

"It's too soon," Thorn said. "She's only been awake a day or so."

"The longer we wait, Brother, the further away the arsonist gets."

"It's all right, Thorn. I have a few things to say," Phyllida said.

Sandy left and Thorn took the dinner tray. He was unprepared for the next question. "May I have a mirror?"

Edith hastily left, brushing the tears from her cheeks. "Poor girl," she murmured under her breath. She stopped Sandy and sheriff at the stairs. "Give her a minute, Mr. Sandy."

Sandy nodded with understanding and redirected the sheriff to the library where Edith brought them coffee.

Thorn hesitated for a moment before giving Phyllida the mirror.

Phyllida stared at herself in disbelief.

A section of hair, behind her ear, was singed and matted. She could see that her ear was severely burnt. Fortunately, her face was untouched, aside from the smoke that had caused her eyes to swell, but her neck and shoulder were badly burned.

She would always have the scars.

"I'm…I'm so sorry, Phyllida," Thorn said softly.

"It's not your fault, Thorn. I'm healthy, and I have people who care for me— " she pushed the mirror away. Her ear looked so black and crusted.

" —people who love you," Thorn corrected as he clasped her hand.

She smiled. "Why fret the silly things in life? I'll wear my hair down for awhile until this singed section grows out," she said, touching the matted hair with slight disdain. "Oh dear, it does look bad."

"You're trying to be brave."

"Perhaps I am. But I refuse to crumble and cry over a small section of missing hair. Fortunately, I was burned in a place that won't be seen too often. That is, if I avoid the gowns you chose for me." She laughed.

"You are a darling woman, Phyllida."

Moments later, Sandy entered her room accompanied by the sheriff and Detective Frodell. Thorn motioned for them to sit as Phyllida folded her hands tightly in her lap. She was sitting next to the windows, her back to the light. She felt lightheaded and her lungs burned, but for a moment she focused on her memory to ensure what had really happened.

"Miss Cowen, how long have you been working for the Langworthys?" the polite sheriff asked.

She answered general questions and at length he asked, "Did you see anyone at the scene?"

Phyllida cleared her burning throat. "I don't recall having seen anyone, but," she paused, "this will sound strange, but I saw someone in my dreams."

"I don't understand."

"I was so frantic when I pushed on the door but it wouldn't move.

I smashed the window and attempted to slip through. There was so much smoke. I was moving quickly, panicked to get out…" Phyllida remembered the sense of contained urgency as she had tried to push herself through the glass. She remembered the glass biting into her flesh, yet it didn't hurt until later. "I was hanging outside the window screaming 'Help!' but the smoke billowed out round me and I couldn't see that well. However, for a moment, I looked up and saw a figure…" She paused again.

"Was it a man? What did he look like?"

"At the time, my mind was running too fast, I was struggling against becoming hysterical, and I looked at him and continued to scream for help. It wasn't until later, in a delirious state, that I actually saw him."

"That could easily be explained as a hallucination," the sheriff gently suggested.

Sandy spoke up. "The mind can witness or hear certain things during a traumatic event. Yet, it won't remember them until some time later. Once when I was a child, I was driving our father's trap much too fast. I ran a sharp curve and plummeted into a tree. I remembered nothing of it until weeks later when I could remember the crash and the scream of the horse."

The sheriff nodded and turned back to Phyllida. "I suppose it is a possibility then. Did you recognize this person?"

"Yes, it was Davis Cleary."

"I knew it!" Thorn hissed. "When I tried to open the door, I saw that it had been purposely rigged to keep anyone from entering, or exiting."

"This is the man you fired some time ago?"

"Yes, and now he's found it in his head to launch solitary attacks on Phyllida. He's trying to get to me through her. First the fallen tree, now this."

"You can't be sure Davis was responsible." The sheriff held up his hand.

"Trees don't chop themselves and attempt to fall on passersby." Thorn scowled.

Detective Frodell said, "I followed my suspicions about Davis and checked around on him. Frank and Davis have crystal clear alibis during the time of the fire."

"Are you sure you saw Davis Cleary?" the sheriff asked Phyllida.

"Yes, I'm very certain. When I screamed, he turned and ran." She frowned and gnawed her lip. "He was standing behind a white pine that was adjacent to the office door, closest to the road. Go back and check, perhaps he dropped something."

"Good idea," the sheriff said, standing up. "I'll have a look around. Until then, I suggest you stay in close company and not go anywhere by yourself."

When they left, Thorn turned to Phyllida. "Again, I'm so sorry…"

"I've learned a great deal in the last few days," she said.

"What do you mean?"

"I've learned to be grateful for my life, and for what God has given me. I have my health; God allowed me to keep my hair, or most of it—" she smiled, "and even my ear. I learned that I've been blessed with kind people who care for me, especially you. I suppose in time I will work through the small issue of my impaired vanity." She touched her matted hair.

He desperately wanted to hold her again and kiss her like a man possessed, but he held back. He needed to sort out the Cleary affair first. His biggest problem was getting Cleary before he could get to Phyllida.

The next several weeks passed without notice. Phyllida felt rehabilitated and wanted to begin working again. Thorn gave in and Phyllida spent her days in the library sorting various papers and writing letters to prospective business associates. She stayed busy, almost distracted as if she wanted to distance herself from the horrible episode. Thorn loitered about, always ready to lend a hand. Sandy and Lewis continued supervising the final stages at the sites. Thorn completely let his thoughts about work fade because Phyllida was his main concern.

One afternoon Sandy told Thorn about several dozens of logs that had been stolen. "Even with the Langworthy brand, the thieves still took them. There must be an organized slew of them to get away with so much lumber."

"Believe it or not, that is of minimal importance to me. At one time I would have wanted to kill whoever was on watch duty, but now...things are different."

"I'm glad, Brother. Truly I am. Are you and Phyllida still planning a wedding in a few weeks?"

"I haven't talked to her about it, but I'm guessing she may not want to right now because of her scars. I know that sounds odd, but I can't blame her. She has to wear her hair down and is slightly self-conscious about the burns."

"I understand."

"Be prepared, Brother. The estate and business may not be ours after all. I'm only sorry for you and Lewis."

"No Thorn, it's all right. I suppose I'll miss the acreage and the opportunity to build my own home. But there are more important things in life."

"Yes, more important things—like Phyllida," he said, thinking of her beautiful face and thick long hair. "I rather like her disheveled look."

"You have really changed," Sandy mused.

"I feel changed. I don't know where the anger went, or the obsession over money and power. It's gone...maybe because I realize I am nothing without God. I am nothing."

Phyllida had just finished the last of Thorn's correspondences and sealed the envelopes. She rubbed at her inky, tired hands and sighed. How good it felt to be active again! she thought.

Suddenly she had the feeling she was being watched. Instinctively she looked out the window and thought she saw the shrubs move slightly. As she moved to investigate, Thorn came into the library and closed the door.

"Is something wrong?" Thorn asked from behind her.

She turned, startled. "You frightened me!"

"I hope I never frighten you, Phyllida," he said, smiling.

Her heart rushed at the sight of him. He was wearing a grey suit, and had removed his tie, revealing his dark neck. She found herself looking at the small divot in his neck where it pulsed slightly with every one of his heartbeats. She turned away quickly. "I finished the letters to your solicitors and the three to the prospective investors."

"Thank you." He followed her to the desk.

He gently touched her arm and drew her to the fire. For a moment neither spoke. She looked up at him, seeing Thorn as a new man. His dark eyes searched her face, yearning for her.

"Phyllida," he said huskily, "I...I don't know how to begin to say this..." He clasped her hands.

"My hands are inky." She tried to draw away but his grasp tightened.

"I don't care."

His eyes searched her face for acceptance. He noted the natural line from her nose to her mouth. He admired her high cheekbones and the way her eyes unwavering looked into his own with confidence. How he wanted to kiss her, touch her jaw line, her chin and ears! He wanted to feel his lips on her delicate eyelids and the way her thick lashes pressed against her cheek when she looked downward. He loved her immensely and felt so unworthy of her devotion.

"Considering the circumstances," he glanced at the purple burns on her neck, "I think we should cancel the winter social. Further, the wedding should be canceled until spring."

"Why?"

"I thought you would prefer to wait, due to..." He glanced at the matted hair.

"Thorn, why should our lives cease because of this?"

"But— "

"Dearest, I never imagined anyone would ever love me. Then I came to know the Lord and I have found a love beyond all of my understanding. Now the Lord has allowed me to experience the love between a man and a woman. I am so grateful," she said.

"Always humble," he murmured, pulling her into his arms again. He rested his chin on her soft hair as she molded herself against him.

Little did they realize two pairs of eyes watched from behind the shrubs. Davis Cleary whispered to his brother, "She's a tough one to finish, but I'm not giving up."

"Why, Davis? Why her?" Frank asked.

Davis didn't speak at first, but then said, "I used to envision destroying Thorn Langworthy for the money hungry person that he is. But that's an easy out for him. Instead, I want to destroy the most important person in his life. Then he can know what it's like to live with grief and despair. He'll think twice about altering people's lives."

Frank did not reply, but watched the two lovers talking with energy, their hands clasped in mutual affection.

Chapter 6

Maisy and Betty twittered around Phyllida. "Why, that dress is stunning! It fits like a charm. You've outdone yourself Maisy."

"I am very pleased with the gown," Phyllida said as she examined her reflection. Her face flushed slightly. The dress was beautiful and enhanced Phyllida's figure. The powder-blue satin stretched across her small waist and flat stomach. The square collar was opened at the neck, dipping into a modestly scooped bodice. The height of the collar was not in fashion, Maisy had warned, but it was the best she could do to design something that covered Phyllida's healing scars. Gathered at the bosom was a deep blue flower. "I made the flower one night. Land sakes, it took all night, but it was worth it," Maisy chimed in, admiring her workmanship.

The women did not notice the customer who had entered the shop and was watching Phyllida's fitting with slight impatience.

Betty glanced over her shoulder. "I'll be with you in a minute, ma'am."

"Shall I go elsewhere?" came the reply.

The women turned, surprised by her rudeness. Phyllida said quietly, "I've taken so much of your time. Excuse me." She parted to the dressing room to remove the gown.

Maisy, who was slightly flustered, asked, "What can I do for you, ma'am?"

"I need a gown, something that can be altered immediately."

"I see," Betty said, grabbing her pencil and pad.

The woman proceeded to give her measurements as well as the desired cut and style of the gown. Maisy realized the woman had been in her store weeks prior.

"Tell me," the woman asked Maisy, "is that the Langworthy trap outside?"

"Why, yes. Thorn has brought his fiancée in," Maisy nodded towards the dressing room, "and is probably off to do some business himself."

"His fiancée?" the other woman asked in a slight whisper.

"Yes," Betty replied, eager to share any town gossip. "They're announcing their engagement at the Langworthys' winter social."

"When is the social?" she asked quietly.

"Tomorrow night," Betty said excitedly. "We all have new dresses to wear! There hasn't been a social in ages."

"Thank you, Maisy and Betty." Phyllida smiled as she carried the garment out with her. "Are we all settled then?"

"Yes, you're all paid up, Miss Phyllida. I could have simply billed Mr.Thorn for you."

"No, I've paid for the dress myself," she said, smiling happily. Then turning to the woman with the icy stare, she nodded warmly. "How do you do? I'm quite sure you'll be in good hands with these ladies."

When she turned the leave, the woman watched her alight the trap, this time accompanying Thorn Langworthy.

"Aren't they a nice couple?" Betty admired. "Her scars are healing up nicely, you can't even see the one behind her ear since she wears her hair down."

"She has certainly been a God-send to Twin Pines," Maisy replied. "Mr. Thorn's a new man."

"Is that so?" the woman replied as she watched Thorn and Phyllida drive away like a story with a happy ending.

That evening, dinner passed gaily. The brothers were laughing, reminiscing about stories from their youth. Phyllida dabbed at her eyes. "My sides are hurting! What naughty boys you were!"

Lewis sighed. "They were good times, weren't they? It's a wonder Mother didn't box our ears and send us off to England to live with our relatives. She was so patient."

Sandy smiled. "We gave her many headaches. Brother, do you remember the time…" he went on as the doorbell sounded and Edith opened the door. The brothers and Phyllida laughed aloud again; even Annie and Bella, who brought dessert, enjoyed the stories of their youth.

"Bella, the soup was excellent," Thorn said before turning back to Lewis's story.

"Mother was sitting down to luncheon with several businessmen's wives. It was a formal affair but I was allowed to sit in."

Sandy chimed in, "I bought some fireworks from a peddler. The old peddler said they would just make a snap noise…but far from it! I definitely got my money's worth and more!"

"I'll never forget it; the women were sipping their soup so prim and proper when an explosion echoed throughout the house. They dropped their spoons and glasses—and their manners. They screamed, 'Canon ball! Canon ball! The South has risen again! The rebels are coming!'"

"I hid under the table doubled over in laughter. Mother, who was always calm, settled them down and sent Edith to investigate the attic. That's when she brought down Sandy, by his ear. He was covered in soot, his hair awry. The damage had been done, the culprit found out."

They laughed heartily and Thorn looked up to see Edith. She was white-faced but Sandy, who didn't notice, asked, "Do you remember that, Edith? You twisted my ear so hard that I offered to give you some of the fireworks if you'd stop."

He laughed but when she didn't answer, Thorn asked, "What is it, Edith?"

"There's a visitor here, sir."

"Send him in then," Thorn said, waving toward the door.

"She is here to see you, sir." She nodded a warning glance at Thorn.

"Well, send her in then."

Edith paused and was about to protest when a woman slid past her. She was tall and slender, almost too slender, and was dressed beautifully in a dark blue traveling habit with a smart hat with plume feathers arched across her head. Phyllida recognized her as the unfriendly woman from Maisy's dress shop.

The woman looked only at Thorn who, like Edith, had gone white.

No one spoke.

Phyllida rose and moved towards the woman. "Welcome to Twin Pines. I am Phyllida Cowen. Can I offer you— "

"I'm Clarice Moss."

"What a lovely name! I believe I saw you earlier today." Phyllida glanced behind her saying, "Allow me to introduce you, Miss Moss. This is..."

"I know everyone here, except you of course." She turned her icy glance over Phyllida's plain dress.

"I see." She wondered why no one spoke. Thorn rose and Phyllida asked Annie to bring a cup of tea and an extra place setting.

"I will not be here long," the woman said, watching Thorn.

"It's been a long time," he finally replied.

"Indeed."

Phyllida, who was unaffected by the cool demeanor, asked, "May I offer you anything, Miss Moss?"

"You may not," she said without looking at her.

"Perhaps we could speak privately," Thorn said.

"What I have to say will be said to everyone, especially her." She nodded at Phyllida.

Phyllida glanced between them, bewildered.

"Tell her who I am," Clarice said.

"You are a former friend of mine," he said with his eyes resuming the dark unfathomable stare.

Lewis looked down at his plate and Sandy stared at an invisible spot on the wall.

"Is that what I am?" she said with forced laughter.

"I don't understand, Thorn," Phyllida said quietly.

"Let me explain then," Clarice said, turning her baleful stare at Phyllida. She thrust out her thin hand where upon her finger sparkled a large sapphire ring.

Phyllida was unprepared for the stranger's next words: "I am Thorn's fiancée."

Thorn was grateful that his brothers promptly escorted themselves, along with Phyllida, from the dining room. He couldn't help but see the confusion and concern in Phyllida's weak smile. Once again, she had faith in Thorn and was trying to be strong. When the door closed, he turned on Clarice. "What are your motives for returning? I thought you had married and moved to Detroit."

Clarice shrugged. "I married a month after you returned to Michigan. My husband died three years ago and didn't leave me a penny. It was all over gossip columns," she said bitterly.

"And now life's gotten troublesome without the comfortable lifestyle your husband afforded you," Thorn said, noting that she had not changed a great deal. Clarice was beautiful, but icy.

Faint lines appeared around her eyes as she scowled. "You always think the worst of me, Thorn."

"Am I correct?" he persisted.

"Look," she said, "let's cut to the chase. It doesn't matter what life was like for me. What matters is I've come here to make you honor your obligations."

"Such as…"

"Marriage to me."

"I'm to be married to Phyllida," he said with determination.

"It seems I've come just in time then."

"You don't understand." Thorn's voice dropped. "I won't marry you. Not now, not ever."

She held up a faded yellow letter. He instantly recognized his handwriting. "Of course you won't deny me when I show the world this letter, which reads," she paused to read, holding the paper close to her face. He guessed her to be nearsighted. "'I will forever obligate myself to you, even if you turn down my proposal for matrimony. I will love you, and only you forever. To this I pledge my love and undying devotion, my dearest Clarice Moss.'" She looked up, the gleam of triumph in her eyes. "I will show this letter to the press—more specifically, the gossip columns. I know firsthand how gossip writers can completely destroy reputations. Your famous lumber mill and precious family name can do without the mud slinging."

"I was twenty-one, Clarice! I was foolish!" Thorn shouted. "And what of Phyllida?"

"I couldn't care less about that silly girl. She's young…she'll marry someone else and forget all about you."

"What kind of financial trouble are you having?" he asked impulsively as he walked to his desk. He pulled out cheques bearing the family crest. "I will pay you what you want if you'll agree to leave—forever."

"That won't do. You see," she paused, "my husband Charles afforded me a lifestyle and a status that I cannot compromise."

"Why doesn't that surprise me?"

She ignored him. "Marry me or pay dearly." It seemed she was flashing the unspoken trump card.

"You make this so tempting," he scorned, the old angry Thorn returning.

"I could make life quite uncomfortable for you. Think of all those business investors and customers hearing of such a scandal— "

"Hush!"

"Easy does it, Thorn," she whispered in mock sincerity. She tipped her head to one side and said, "You've changed, Thorn. I can't put my finger on it, but you've changed. If you don't do what I ask, the story will be run in next week's paper. I can see the headline now: 'Lumber Mill Tycoon Betrays Fiancée'" Then under her breath she added, "…in more ways than one."

"No one will believe it," he hissed.

She raised her eyebrows. "Do you really want to find out?" she inquired, her question laced with threat. I'll be back tomorrow." Then seeing his look, she continued. "Yes, you heard me. I'll be a guest at your winter social tomorrow night, so don't try anything silly, Thorn."

Thorn pulled the bell rope and Edith appeared. "Show this person to the door," he said icily.

"I have a name, you know," she retorted.

"I've been trying to forget it for the last sixteen years."

When she left, Thorn went to the library where he drank a pot of tea. His mouth was parched and his hands trembled. It seemed his worst nightmare was coming true.

Sandy quietly let himself in and clasped his hands behind his back. "Well? What now, Brother?"

"Don't let me see the disappointment in your eyes," he half pleaded, exhausted.

Sandy shook his head. "I'm not disappointed in you. No doubt, you've gotten yourself into a quandary with her, but I'm unclear why she's here and what she wants. "

Thorn didn't answer his brother's implied question. "How well do you remember Clarice?"

Sandy frowned then shrugged. "I recall meeting her for just a few moments nearly sixteen years ago. It seems Father wasn't too impressed with her, but Lewis and I thought she was gorgeous. But within weeks, she disappeared and you never spoke of her again. What is really going on?"

"I'll explain everything to you and Lewis, but first, tell me how Phyllida is holding up."

"She handled herself like a lady. She didn't ask any questions, but went quietly to her room."

Thorn recalled how her face had gone pale, her lashes looking strangely dark against her pale skin as she looked down at her hands. She neither pressed Clarice or Thorn to explain themselves, but withdrew with Sandy and Lewis. Why didn't she stay and demand him to address this woman's strange claims? Instead she left him standing before the woman he, at one time, thought he loved passionately. How fleeting his passion was compared to his steadfast yet burning love for Phyllida! It was all sounding like a gothic romance gone awry.

"Where do I begin? How could I have known that such recklessness would land me in this predicament?"

"On second thought, I think you should explain this to Phyllida first. She deserves to hear this more than anyone."

"Will you send for her?"

Sandy left and Thorn turned towards the fire, his hands still damp with perspiration. He felt sick having to relive his foolish past, but it seemed that buried secrets have a way of unearthing themselves only to haunt. "Why, Lord?" he murmured. Where was God? He drew a deep breath and murmured a small prayer. "Please release me from the bonds of the past. I beg for your forgiveness, Lord, for my horrible sin, the sin I must confess to Phyllida. Let me have a second chance, Lord." Then he sighed, "Despite my pleas, it must be Your will and no other way."

The door closed softly and he turned to look at Phyllida. She was wearing a pale pink gown, her hair loose as if she was preparing for bed. A silk ribbon held back her hair, her lips similarly pink smiled at him with what seemed to be courage.

"You are a portrait of beauty and grace."

"Thorn," she began, but caught herself as tears welled in her eyes.

"Oh Phyllida, what have I done?" He crossed the room and caught her in his arms. "Let me explain," he said, trying to ignore the knot in his stomach.

She moved past him and sat, her hands clutched on her lap. Without looking at her, he began to speak. "What Clarice said was true. I proposed to her when I was twenty-one—and she accepted. But there is more to the story that you should know..."

Thorn's father had sent him to Wisconsin for a few months to study various lumbering methods under the tutelage of a prosperous lumber tycoon. While in Madison, he attended a high-class social event with the tycoon's family. He couldn't remember if it was a fundraiser, or some sort of social ball. But he did remember seeing a young, beautiful girl who seemed to captivate every man in the room. He remembered how stunning she was then. Clarice Moss was chic, stylish and cultured. She laughed gracefully and smiled flirtatiously without overdoing either trait. She had been poised and polished for high society by her father, a local politician. Thorn later learned that her father was in debt up to his ears due to bad financial investments. He wished he had known that sooner, he explained to Phyllida.

They talked all night, he remembered. She asked him all about his business, the estate, his title in the company. He was astounded by her shrewd interest in the business. Strangely, their affection hastily bloomed into a relationship. She confessed that she had heard of him, as Langworthy Lumber was becoming one of the greatest lumber businesses in the country. He was even briefly featured in the national newspapers' "who's who" columns. Clarice's father seemed to view Thorn with a sigh of relief, almost as if his problems were over thanks to Thorn's family name. Then as his study neared its end, she asked him with unusual boldness, "When will you ask me to marry you?" He sensed an internal warning at such a question asked—the answer almost assumed—by the debutante. But Thorn shoved aside his thoughts and plunged forward blindly. They were engaged and the newspapers covered the event with excitement, while Clarice's father smiled with relief mixed with greed.

But upon meeting Clarice, Thorn's father privately expressed his concern. "Engagements can be broken, but marriage is a sealed deal."

"Spoken like a true businessman," Thorn had said lightly.

"I'm very serious, Thorn. Something is amiss with the lass. Don't be blinded by her beauty. Tell me, did you propose to her, or did she propose to you?"

Thorn didn't answer, but concealed his own concern with more smiles and talk of the happy future he felt certain they would have. Deep inside he was inclined to take towards his father's advice, but before he could act upon it, he was whisked away by her beauty and charm.

"What happened next?" Phyllida asked. Thorn realized he had paused too long. He went on to explain that their wedding plans had come to a halt one beautiful afternoon as they were picnicking.

"Will I be able to redecorate when we return to Twin Pines?"

Thorn thought for a moment. "Ah, I'm glad you mentioned that. I need to write my father and ask him to see that renovation begins at the cottage. It overlooks the most beautiful ravines…"

"What cottage?"

"The cottage I had told you about. It's small, but homey— "

"A cottage?" she said, barely swallowing a piece of apple. "I thought I was to live at Twin Pines?" Her eyes turned to green ice.

"Why did you think we'd live there? I told you—Twin Pines is my father's home. Am I to turn them out of doors?"

"You own the company, so why not? Why can't he live at the cottage?"

"I don't own the company! Say—where did you get such ideas?"

"I thought…" she sputtered, "I thought you owned Langworthy Lumber. You seemed to know so much about running the business, the stock, Twin Pines…" she rambled.

"Of course, because one day it will all be mine, but I cannot expect to turn my family out of Twin Pines while my father owns every square inch of Langworthy Lumber."

"I thought you said he was ill."

"Indeed, he's ailing, but only from age. He will live a long time to be sure!" He was startled by her hopefulness. "You act as if his ill health is to your benefit."

"Well, yes, it is to my benefit!" she spat furiously. "I've let you woo me and waste my time like this only to find that I will live as a scullery maid? I shall not! You've misled me, Thorn Langworthy!"

The last shell of his adolescence dropped away and he saw her for what she was. In a moment his world went from one filled with love and romance, to one of pain and resentment. "I did no such thing, you foolish woman! This is the package!" He pointed at himself. "How dare you waste my time! You only wanted to marry me for status and money. Well, even if I had the money now that will one day be mine, I certainly wouldn't waste it on a silly frock like you!"

What he thought was love had quickly evaporated into hatred. She glared back. "Well, now look at this change in demeanor! Take me home this instant!"

"I hope your father won't be sore about this! After all, how will he take care of his debts?"

"How dare you! A lady is not to know of such things!"

"You're not a lady, but a bad attempt at a debutante."

Clarice slapped him across the face. "You're nothing, Thorn Langworthy, not now, not ever. I felt sorry for you the night I met you. You were so Midwestern with your silly British twang."

"You didn't feel sorry for me. You came after me just to get your hand into the Langworthy money jar," he retorted, feeling calmer.

For a moment, she did not speak. He could see that she was thinking quickly and it was at that moment his world went from bad to worse.

"This is a fine predicament," she said in a low voice. "What will I do about the baby?"

The earth seemed to stop despite the singing birds that mocked his horror.

"What?" he gasped.

"You heard me," she said, throwing the half eaten apple. "What are we going to do about the baby?"

"I didn't know… I didn't realize— "

"You insipid, backwoods boy! Did you not think anything would result from our affection?"

"I— " he began.

"I'll manage," she said, strangely calm—almost too calm.

"But it's my child." He glanced at her slender waist. "Now you have to marry me."

She shook her head. "And live in a tar-paper shack? No thanks—my child deserves better."

"No! What can I do?" he nearly begged. Thorn had never liked children, and for that matter, never cared for women. But all at once he recognized the burden of his responsibility. The child was his and both child and mother had to be cared for.

"Send your father and brothers to live at the Ravines. Ask him for fifty percent of the company in your name. Then I shall consider marrying you…for the sake of our child."

He stared at her, not completely internalizing all that she had said.

First he was a father, second, he must discard his own father? "How can I do that to them all?"

"Your family will have to make room for our family." She flicked a speck of dust from her lap. "It's that simple."

Just when he thought he was almost free he climbed back into her cage, but this time he wasn't blinded by lust. He looked again at her small waist. She showed no sign of pregnancy, but then, what did he know of such matters? She seemed to read his thoughts. "You're a fool, Thorn Langworthy."

Thorn's father had taught him about such relationships. Though their talk had been embarrassing, Old Mr. Langworthy was direct and purposeful: "That is to be saved for marriage, for your wife." But he had been so young and foolish. How he regretted barely listening to his father's invaluable honesty!

"Please be reasonable. We will have all that we need at the Ravines— " he began.

She rose. "I never want to see you again."

"Let me come back…to visit the child."

She held up her hand. "I expect you to go away nicely—if you don't, I could make things horrible for you."

"What do you mean?"

"What I mean is— " she stopped short, exasperated. "Bringing an illegitimate child into the world and then abandoning me? I could twist this tale to make you look the criminal. Of course, I can't afford to look wanton either, but if I go down, you're coming with me."

"What do you want?" he asked, thinking how such shame would disappoint his father.

"I want money—enough to cover my father's excessive debts. Then I want you to go away and leave me alone. Don't contact me, and don't have me followed."

"But the baby— "

"Forget the baby!" she hissed. "I shouldn't have told you anyway!"

"Don't do this," he pleaded.

Clarice turned her icy eyes and glared balefully at him. "You have an easy way out of this, so take it while I'm feeling generous. I hold all the cards, Thorn—just you remember that! Forget the baby, it doesn't matter anymore. Maybe one day I'll cash in on what you've done to me."

He left Clarice, never to hear from her again. Her father begged and groveled to him, saying "She just doesn't realize what kind of wealth you'll have one day." Mr. Moss obviously knew nothing of her "condition" or he would have probably shot Thorn. One month after the feud, Thorn received word that Clarice had married an older, established gentleman in Detroit. Charles was a widower whose children had all grown. The press covered the wedding with excitement. Thorn expected his name to be mentioned, but Charles's wealth and power saw that Clarice's engagement to Thorn was unacknowledged. Though she had never returned the sapphire ring, he considered her finished and forgot all about the trivial detail of the sapphire ring—but never the child, their child.

Phyllida was silent and Thorn went on, "I was nearly sick when she showed me the ring."

"Then there was a double meaning when she said, 'You must honor your promises.'"

He nodded gravely. "I am so sorry, Phyllida. Will I spend the rest of my life saying 'I'm sorry' to you?"

"You were young and foolish," she said, understanding but not excusing his actions.

"That doesn't make it right. Believe me, I've begged God to forgive me so many times. I imagined all kinds of things in the last sixteen years. I guessed the baby to be born in February… I even guessed it was a boy. I figured she named him Charles, after her husband. I wondered what the child looked like, and if he was tall like me…" He was sick with despair. "I've carried this secret around for years, Phyllida. This is one sin I thought I would never have to revisit again. I thought the deep guilt would be payment enough, but it's not."

"You must persuade her to bring the child to you, Thorn. You're obligated to your son or daughter."

"What will everyone say?"

She sighed. "The saying goes, 'People in glass houses shouldn't throw stones…'"

"I see the disappointment in your eyes, just like I did in Sandy's."

"No, Thorn. I love you, but I want you to make right out of this."

"Does that mean I have to marry her?"

Her eyes welded with tears. "If she is the mother of your child, then perhaps."

"I won't!" he shouted, running his hands through his hair.

"Thorn, it may be the right thing to do...isn't it?" she asked, feeling his frustration and confusion. Certainly she loved him and wanted to be his wife, but there was the possibility of a child that belonged to him.

"You would be willing to step aside so I could marry this woman?"

"I would hate it," she began to cry, "but I would do it if it was the right thing to do."

"You'd let me go like that? Like a little bird, you'd fly away from me?" he asked with a faint, sad smile.

"What are my alternatives?" she asked. "Think of this poor child! What kind of life has he or she had with a mother like that? I want you so much, but not at the further expense of an innocent child."

"What if she lied about the child?"

"That may be true, but there are ways of finding out. You must work this through with her."

"Are you saying the wedding is off?"

"It's postponed until the issue is resolved."

"Perhaps if she knew of my father's will and that within weeks I would lose everything..." He looked at Phyllida, "Either way, I will simply lose because I don't have you."

"Clarice is obviously a miserable person. I don't want to see you sentenced to a life with her— Oh, I shouldn't say that! I'm showing my battle with jealousy. It's so hard to do what's right, but I feel this is the most God-honoring thing to do."

"Just when I give over to God, this horror revisits me!" he cried bitterly.

"Dearest," she said, feeling calmer, "ask the Lord what he would have for you to learn here."

"I want to be happy!" he declared. "Isn't Christianity supposed to bring happiness?"

She shook her head. "Being a Christian brings joy, but it doesn't guarantee happiness."

"My mother once told me that, but it seems more brutal coming from you, the greatest joy of my life." He stared at her. "Am I going to lose you?"

"Pray about this, Thorn. There's no other answer."

"Promise me you won't leave until this is sorted out. I need you close by—please."

"This little bird will stay right here," she whispered, caressing his hair. How she longed to throw her arms around him, kiss him wildly and demand that they leave quietly in the night to elope. But that was not reasonable, as they would just be running away from their fears.

"We must carry on as if nothing has happened," Thorn told his brothers and Veronica the next morning.

"He's right," Lewis said. "We cannot cancel the social this late. Why, it starts in six hours! Guests are already coming into town and getting rooms for the night."

"Clarice plans to attend the social tonight."

Veronica gasped, "What about Phyllida?"

"She knows all about this mess. In fact, she knows more about my sordid past than you all." He went on to tell them of the accusation and the probability of being a father.

"Goodness, Thorn! You're lucky Papa never knew of this." Sandy blushed.

"It would have killed him faster than the illness," Thorn replied bitterly. "I already feel responsible enough for rushing him to the grave— "

"That's enough of that, Thorn. I think you have enough crosses to bear," Veronica said.

"Look, just keep an eye on Clarice. I'll deal with her directly after the social. Sandy, I need you to do something for me." He went on to explain the need to telegram a hospital in Detroit. "Find out whatever you can. I need this information tonight, please." Sandy patted his shoulder and quickly let himself out.

Lewis, who had waited patiently asked, "What can I do for you?"

"Always faithful, aren't you, Lewis?" Thorn asked without a trace of his old mockery.

"I want to help."

"Just keep an eye on Clarice. Keep her from doing more damage than she...and I...have already done."

Phyllida and Ruby finished the final touches on the decorations in Twin Pines ballroom. The spacious room was vast with large rectangular windows overlooking the gardens and the lake. Three enormous chandeliers, lowered for dusting, sparkled in the winter sun, sending iridescent prisms throughout the room. In the corner stood a large Christmas tree adorned with tinsel, popcorn strands, cranberry beads, and other trinkets. Clasped to the branches were large white candles pointing upwards where a glass star perched at the top of the tree. The room smelled of pine and cinnamon. A large fireplace roared, gaily warming the usually abandoned room. Phyllida decorated with wide red ribbon along the windows panes, fireplace mantel and doorway to the foyer and dining room. She wanted the atmosphere to be warm and homey, as if two hundred people were coming over to supper. In a similar fashion, Ruby helped Edith prepare a large dinner consisting of roast chicken and beef, potatoes, salads and even fresh fruit and vegetables that had been specially ordered and delivered by an ice car on the last train. "Good home cookin' puts everyone in the right mood," Ruby had said as she inspected the dining room. Bella and Annie laid strands of large, red ribbon down each table. The centerpieces were cleverly arranged with shiny bulbs and pinecones at the base of large silver candelabras.

Veronica had made Ruby aware of Clarice's arrival, and the latter waited patiently for Phyllida to talk about it. Phyllida simmered on nervous energy arranging a vase of poinsettias. She was regarding the Christmas tree and tinkering with a stubborn strand of popcorn when Ruby said, "Come and sit down."

Phyllida pulled one of the chairs from along the wall to sit next to Ruby. "You know what's happened, don't you?"

She nodded. "What do you think of it all?" She patted Phyllida's hand. Phyllida painfully recounted the experience with Clarice, even telling her about the possibility of there being a child.

"I felt so sure that Thorn and I would marry," she said.

Ruby nodded sympathetically. "Let me ask you somethin'." She paused, her usual bluntness more in check than usual. "Do ya suppose…well, how do I ask…do ya suppose there really is a child?"

"I don't know."

Ruby went on, "It sounds like she wants to use the child like a trump card. She won't admit she lied until she gets Thorn."

"Where's my position in all of this?" Phyllida asked. "What is the right thing to do—sit by while Thorn's life closes in around him?"

"Continue lovin' him and prayin' for God's direction," Ruby said, patting Phyllida's arm. "I know yer thinkin' you'd like to take a fryin' pan to her head, but just wait it out. Let God take control."

"I don't feel aggressive towards Clarice," Phyllida corrected her friend. "Rather, I pity her."

"Maybe I'm feelin' that way because I know the pain of losing someone. It's human to want to blame others when things don't go right."

Phyllida sighed and held up her hands. "What does God want me to learn here?"

"Maybe yer not the one who's meant to learn a lesson, but I reckon it's the man ya love."

Phyllida took her time preparing herself for the winter social. Despite her beautiful gown, her previous excitement had dwindled and she lacked the desire to participate. She regarded herself for a moment, focusing on covering the healing scars on her ear and neck. No matter what she did, she just couldn't make them unnoticed without simply pulling her hair around her face. Edith tapped gently on the door and greeted Phyllida. She carried a small basket and closed the door behind her.

"Mr. Thorn is asking for you downstairs."

Phyllida rose to go, but Edith put up her hand. "I told him you'd be a few minutes."

She sat down again and Edith brought over the basket and removed a brush, oils, eye pencils and lipstick.

"Will you give me the honor of dressing that beautiful hair of yours?"

"Yes—you came at the right time! Can you cover my scars?"

"Absolutely." Edith smiled as she began to brush out Phyllida's hair. She rubbed the strands of hair between two silk pads— "It brings out the shine." She sprinkled a few drops of oil as she began to work her wonders. "I used to dress Miss Jenna's hair. She had lovely thick hair like yours, and she always asked me to brush it for her. It gave me great pleasure to do anything for her because she had a giving, kind spirit. Despite her unhappy times, there was always joy in her face."

"Do you believe she loved Mr. Langworthy?"

Edith sighed. "She loved him very much, as he did her. The only difference between the two of them was their priorities. At one time, he loved power and fortune, whereas she always loved God."

"How sad."

"Yes, but eventually he turned his sights around and saw what was really important. Perhaps at the end of his life he pushed Thorn a little hard in a different direction, but he was determined that his son shouldn't make the same mistakes."

"You really love this family, don't you?"

"I do, Miss. And I think of you as one of them. Should things not work out," she paused, "you'll always be dear to me."

"You're very kind." Phyllida blinked.

"Now, don't smudge your makeup. There, what do you think?"

Her hair was coiled into a long twist that ran down her back. The sides, curled with a curling rod, folded along her ears to cover the scars. Her dark eyes were penciled slightly to enhance the thickness of her lashes. Edith had decided against the use of rouge and powders since Phyllida's complexion was like porcelain.

Phyllida looked closely and gasped, "Why, how did you manage such wonders?"

"Years of practice," Edith replied.

Bella knocked, saying, "Mr. Thorn's asking for Miss Phyllida again." She gasped when she saw her mother's handiwork. "You look beautiful, Miss!"

Bella and Edith let themselves out as Phyllida clasped the dainty slippers. She craved to look at herself one last time, but remembered Ada's warning about vanity. She took with her the mental picture of a small woman in a light blue gown that scooped modestly, covering the curves of her shoulders and collarbone. For a moment, she ignored the ugly scar on her ear and neck.

She let herself into the library where she took a moment to regard Thorn. He was looking out the window, his hands clasped behind his back. His proud features stared with uncertainty into the unknown. But when he turned to look at her, the world seemed to temporarily halt.

His eyes warmed with desire when he saw Phyllida. He walked towards her, his face lighting into a smile. "Phyllida you look…"

She met him across the room and went into his arms. She didn't need to hear the words that confirmed the look and the touch she desperately wanted. He grasped her waist and held her against him, her feet light on the ground. He whispered against her hair, "Oh Phyllida…Philly. Will you let me call you Philly when we're an old married couple?" He sighed, breathing in the light lavender scent on her neck. "Oh how I love you, Philly. I love you with all my heart…" He couldn't stand it anymore, he found himself kissing her neck, her ear, even her scar. Then he paused to look into her face, which was moist with tears. "Tell me you love me, Philly. Tell me."

"I love you always," she said, her voice barely a whisper.

Then he kissed her face, murmuring, "Promise me that you won't leave until I sort out this nightmare."

"You can't get rid of me that easily." She laughed softly, modestly embarrassed.

"I hope I didn't muss your hair," he said, laughing lightly.

"I don't care. I want to be beautiful for no one but you and only you."

He groaned and set her on her feet, caressing her hands lovingly before turning around.

"What is it?" she asked, sensing his frustration.

"I want this Clarice affair to be over with. I've carried it for sixteen years. Tonight I had planned to announce our engagement. Now I can't. We're robbed of this joy because of my stupid mistakes."

"Thorn, God makes right out of wrong. You've trusted Him this far, you must see it through. I don't care about engagement announcements, fancy dresses, and elaborate socials. I only want what I see, and that is you."

"Is life always so sure?"

"No, but it helps when we keep things simple."

Then the smile left his face and he asked with a desperate edge in his voice, "What would I do without you? To think I almost let you go and walk out of here when I first met you. Then I think of busting through the fire and groping through the smoke to find your limp hand…" He paused to glance away. "I've never been so sure of my love for anything or anyone as I am of my love for you." He paused to open his desk drawer and take out a small velvet bag. He opened it and took her hand, dropping two small pearl earrings into her palm.

"My earrings! How did you know?"

"Mr. Vincent told me you were in his pawn shop weeks ago. I bought them back for you."

"But I wanted to help— " she began to protest and he put his finger to her lips.

"Wear them tonight and think of the love I have for you."

Somewhere in the distance, the doorbell rang. "That must be some early guests," Phyllida said. "You must greet them, Thorn."

"We will greet them…together."

He took her arm and led her into the great hallway where the portrait of his father went unnoticed for once in his life.

Davis Cleary paced the room, his voice hoarse from shouting. "Don't tell me you're backing out now!"

"Look, this is getting dangerous. You want to kidnap Thorn's fiancée, and for what? To end up in jail for the rest of your life?"

"I'm willing to take that chance, if I'm caught."

Davis settled down next to his brother. They sat before the fire of their small shack. From the window they could hear a banjo playing in the distance. "You can smell the food from Ruby's place," Frank said enviously.

"We're hungry, we're all hungry!" Davis nodded towards his father who snored deeply in the bunk behind them. "And there's nothing we can do about it, not while Mr. High-n-Mighty throws his winter socials and keeps working his men into the ground."

"But I've heard there have been some real improvements— "

"Hush, Frank. You've always been too soft for your own good." Then, leaning his elbows on his knees, Davis said, "I want to clip his wings, make his life difficult."

"I don't want to be a part of it. She's a nice girl, and doesn't have anything to do with your hatred for Thorn Langworthy."

"What about Pa? He's been a good pa our whole life and now it's our turn to take care of him. He has to pitch manure while you and me are milking cows at Grostin's farm for a nickel a day."

"We would have had our jobs if you hadn't hollered at Thorn."

Davis' eyes narrowed. "I'm warning you, Frank. I need your help, and Pa needs your help. If you let me down, you're not my brother. My plan is simple: we kidnap the girl and leave a ransom note. I promise she won't be harmed."

"You tried to kill her twice already," he said disbelievingly.

"I was angry then. Now I've settled down. I want to get some money out of this."

"If I help, do you promise not to hurt her?"

Davis smiled, holding up his hands in mock innocence. "Now, what kind of man do you take me for?"

Frank didn't reply.

The music was intoxicating, Phyllida thought.

An orchestra played various classical pieces, Christmas carols and hymns as guests lingered with punch glasses. She admired the gowns of rich satin crèmes, ruby red, deep blue, and pale yellows all complimented by dazzling diamond earrings and tiaras. Phyllida glanced at Thorn, who was visited with long lost friends. Occasionally he glanced over to smile at Phyllida. She noted his eyes darted over the room as if he were searching with dread. She knew he was guarded and prepared for the worst as Clarice had not yet arrived. Phyllida was soon swept away by the gaiety of the evening. She was introduced to various people who were eager to meet the pretty young woman.

Thorn, on the other hand, barely heard his guests. He smiled politely but watched for Sandy. When he caught his glance, Sandy shook his head as if to say, "Not yet, Brother. Be patient." How he depended on him at that moment!

"Brother," Lewis whispered.

"Yes, what is it?" Thorn turned.

"She's here."

"What?"

"Over there." Lewis subtly nodded in the direction of the hall entrance. "She is asking for you and being quite loud about it."

"I see," he said. "Has a messenger arrived yet?"

"Not that I'm aware of, but rest assured that Sandy's waiting."

"Tell him that I'll be in the library with Clarice."

Lewis nodded and moved away. It seemed the brothers moved like puppets, determined not to show their anxiety in front of their guests.

Thorn's stomach lurched when he saw Clarice. She was dressed in a velvet green gown with mink trim around the scooped neck and sleeves. Her hair was piled beautifully in the latest fashion as her green eyes blazed eagerly for Thorn.

As a Christmas carol came to its end, Edna rang the dinner bell. Thorn moved to the great fireplace and asked everyone for silence as he offered a prayer of thanks. He cleared his throat, ignoring the dryness of his mouth. Just by offering a public prayer of thanks for the food and for the safe arrival of guests, Thorn felt his spirit ease. Upon the hearty amen's, Thorn confidently directed guests to the dining room. He followed the crowd into the adjoining room where three long tables were laid out with roasted chicken and beef carvings. Another table hosted warm buttered rolls, fruits and vegetables. The last table displayed Ruby's chocolate, apple and huckleberry pies, and Bella's chocolate sheet cakes. Older guests furnished their plates to eat at the tables where candlelight glistened over the polished silver. The younger, more energetic guests sat in groups, balancing dinner plates on their knees. Phyllida ate with Lewis who chatted gaily about how good it was to have fresh fruit and vegetables in the dead of winter. "What a nice social," he said, trying to be lighthearted.

She agreed as she glanced around for Thorn. He and Clarice were nowhere to be seen.

"He planned on this being an engagement party. I'm only sorry that he was prevented from making the announcement. I sure wish this ordeal was over for the both of you."

"Everything will work out, Lewis," Phyllida said.

"You really gave him a chance, Phyllida. No one else would have put up with his moods, and you even forgave him when he admitted to bringing you here under false pretenses. He wasn't very honest at first."

"He's a changed man."

"Thanks to you," Lewis consented.

"No, thanks to God. Without Him nothing, absolutely nothing, is redeemable."

Lewis paused. "You're right. It's been a long time since I've had an intimate relationship with God. Mother used to be the spiritual leader here, but when she became ill…"

"You were close to her, weren't you?"

He nodded. "She didn't baby me like Thorn teases. We were close because we had a lot in common. She recognized that I wasn't a businessman like my father and I think it relieved her. Ironically, it disappointed my father and Thorn."

"What about Sandy?"

"He accepts me no matter what. He's sort of the good balance between us all, being the calm, all-accepting brother. I think we wore him out at times with our varying personalities, but Sandy remains steadfast in his faith. He doesn't give a whit about wealth and power. I like that about him. You know, Thorn is becoming a lot like that too. I don't think he cares either way if he loses Langworthy Lumber and Twin Pines as long as he has you."

Thorn's anxiety turned to weariness.

Clarice and Thorn had argued for what seemed hours. At first Clarice begged him to take her back. She pleaded with her eyes, then grasped his hand. "Touch my hair. Remember the way you used to like how it smelled?"

He pulled away and moved towards the library. From across the hallway, he could see the ballroom where guests were finishing dinner. He saw Phyllida and Lewis talking. There was no sign of Sandy.

"Still thinking of your little Brit?" she asked, following his gaze.

"I think you should go. You're obviously too excited to talk this out."

"Do you realize what you're doing to me?" she said. "I could give you so much, more than that little slip of a girl could."

"What are you talking about?"

"Haven't you noticed what a little thing she is? Women that size die all the time in childbearing. She's not very stylish either; her dress looks so plain and drab. I suppose it suits her since she's rather plain anyway— "

"Get out!" he hissed. "We've done nothing but argue for the last half hour. I would have hoped you would tell me about the child, but I see this conversation is focused on your needs."

"You'll never see your son, not until you marry me."

"I'll show you the door."

They made their way into the corridor where guests were finishing dinner. To his dismay, she jerked her arm from his grip and said, "What's it going to be? Are you marrying me or not?"

"Since you insinuate that I have an option, then I gladly say no, I will not marry you."

"Don't tell me no! I'll force your hand! I'll make you marry me, Thorn Langworthy!"

"You're mad," he hissed. "I truly think you're insane."

"Think of your son, your boy who has your dark eyes and nice hair."

"Tell me his name," he said eagerly.

"Tell your guests that I am your fiancée," she said deliberately.

"Never."

"Do it, and enjoy a long life with your son, heir to the Langworthy fortune."

"I can't marry you even if I was insane enough to do so," he said, withdrawing a copy of his father's will. "My father left a contingency in his will that I should marry a woman of British birth within a year of his death. You, Clarice, are not of British birth."

She paused for a moment as if deliberating her next move. "I am not a fool, Thorn Langworthy. A man of your financial prowess has a little savings tucked away. You'll not convince me that you'll be broke."

"But I will no longer own Langworthy Lumber or Twin Pines," he said, baiting her.

Clarice glared at him shrewdly. "I don't care about either at the present. What I need is a secure family name, something that tells the world that Clarice Moss married into a famous family. I need the name, Thorn."

"Why?" he asked, exasperated.

"You can't imagine how savage the press can be to a person who slips past society's definition of perfection." She paused. "Thorn, you cannot betray me."

Thorn glanced around for Sandy. Where was he? He needed him more than ever.

Phyllida forced herself to proceed with the night's festivities. She saw Ruby and Irving talking together most of the evening. At one point, Ruby grasped her arm and whispered, "Don't think I don't know how foolish I look in this garb, but Irv says I'm pretty as a peacock." She winked. Ruby's velvet blue dress was high collared with a pressed waist that fell into rich folds around her legs. Her hair had been curled with a rod around her angular face. Her eyes looked particularly blue and her complexion was flushed with pleasure and confidence.

"I'm used to seeing you in a linen skirt and soiled apron." Phyllida gazed at her friend. "You truly look lovely tonight." Ruby waved her compliments aside as Irving reclaimed her. The couple moved away, absorbed in one another.

Maisy, who had been watching Ruby and Irving, asked Phyllida, "What do you think of my creation?"

"You do wonders with a needle," Phyllida said in admiration.

"I've done most of the gowns here tonight," she beamed. "With Betty's help, of course."

Phyllida smiled and Maisy went on, "If you get any compliments, which I am sure you will since you look so beautiful, tell them I'm your designer and where they can find me."

Maisy excused herself to continue her inspection of her artwork. Eventually, Phyllida withdrew from the lively chatter and energetic music to steal away in the library. She sat on one of the morning seats of the tall windows. She stared outside, marveling at the cold night. The trees glistened in the moonlight and the snow sparkled from the harsh but beautiful winter. She stared at her reflection, noting that she had lost some of her color and looked tired. Veronica, who had seen Phyllida steal away, followed her.

"How are you holding up, m'dear?"

Phyllida turned. "Oh Veronica, I didn't see you there. I'm doing well, but growing tired—and there's no sign of guests growing weary! Perhaps it's the Christmas spirit."

Veronica, in her usual red velvet, sat in a chair facing her. "I saw Clarice visiting with guests, but I can't seem to find Thorn anywhere. It's hard to wait, isn't it?"

She nodded. "I trust Thorn to work this out as he sees fit, but I admit that I am a little uncomfortable with her presence. I wish he didn't have to endure such trouble."

"It will sound cold, but I think Thorn needs this experience."

"What do you mean?"

"As you know, Thorn is a complex creature. His moods are unpredictable, stormy—anything but settled. He's had a way of getting himself in and out of trouble with few scrapes. Clarice represents a part of his past that has caught up with him. He must stand on his own two feet and take his medicine. He didn't do right by Clarice either. Mind you, he was young and somewhat stupid as we all can be in our youth." She winked. "He'll pull through, but right now he needs the Lord. He's never had to depend on anyone before."

"Where do I fit into all of this?"

"It's simple. You're the goal he's trying to reach. He wants you and only you. But he knows that he cannot have what he wants, not yet anyway. 'Let patience have her perfect work…'" she quoted. "That's what you have to do, m'dear."

Thorn was relieved when Clarice became caught up in conversation with one of his business associate's wife. They began to chat about silks and various Parisian styles coming out in the spring. This would be his life with her, he thought. He had never once heard Phyllida discuss frocks, hairstyles, or jewelry. He was the one who pressed her to wear newer, more fashionable clothing. How shallow he had been! Why did he try to change her? Phyllida was beautiful tonight, but she was just as beautiful in her faded, cotton morning dress.

Suddenly he caught sight of Sandy, who motioned Thorn into the hallway. Thorn withdrew but not without attracting Clarice's baleful glance. "Don't go far, Thorn," she called out after him.

Sandy held the telegram, it's thin paper gleaming like a precious diamond.

"It's as you thought, Brother. Congratulations."

Chapter 7

Thorn found Phyllida and Veronica in the library.

"You look as bright as a Christmas tree, Thorn. What are you up to?" Veronica laughed.

He held a slip of paper in his fingers. "This is my ticket," he said, and then looked at Phyllida. "This is our ticket. Stay here, I'll join you shortly."

"This is my cue to leave." Veronica leaned over and kissed Phyllida's forehead.

Thorn reached Clarice, who asked anxiously, "Where have you been?"

"Meet me in the library," he said.

Clarice went to the library and found Phyllida there alone.

The two women regarded each other solemnly. Clarice was pretty, but Phyllida thought she also looked angry. Her green eyes were piercing, shrewd and suspicious. Her nose was small as were her lips. She already showed signs of premature lines along her mouth not so much from age, but from bitterness. Phyllida extended her hand. "Hello, Clarice."

Clarice glanced over Phyllida and said, "Hello, Philda."

"My name is Phyllida," she gently corrected, and then rushed on, "Would you like some tea?"

"Thorn will be with me shortly, so you can go."

"He's asked me to meet him here as well."

"I wonder what he's up to," Clarice said.

"Please," Phyllida paused, "I don't want us to be enemies."

Clarice's cool eyes assessed Phyllida and said calmly, "You're not as pretty as I thought you'd be. That style of dress must be ten years old...."

Phyllida flushed but before she could reply, a deep voice said, "I think she's the most beautiful creature I've ever laid eyes on."

Clarice and Phyllida spun around to see Thorn standing in the shadow of the doorway.

"How sticky sweet." She rolled her eyes, and then turned to Phyllida. "I think I'll take that tea after all, Philda."

Thorn began to protest, but Phyllida subtly shook her head and excused herself.

She reached the kitchens and asked Edith to prepare a tray. Edith replied, "I don't like the looks of her, Miss. She has us awful nervous."

"Everything will be fine." Phyllida smiled reassuringly.

Edith bustled past her murmuring something about Clarice riding in on a broomstick. Phyllida loitered about the kitchen and for a moment, her gaze rested on the small nook where she and Thorn had sat through the night. Her heart lurched remembering the way his hair was tousled and his wide eyes gazing at her with warmth.

Phyllida was a little afraid of Clarice Moss and what she could do to their future. Though she kept praying for a stronger trust in the Lord, Phyllida found herself taking back the burden of her worries. One moment she gave up her concerns, another moment she took them back, wanting to manage them her way. It was if the Lord was gently telling her, "Stop wrestling with these burdens. Give them to me. Trust me." Still, she couldn't give them up.

Clarice looked up when Phyllida entered the library. "Does she have to be here?"

"She is to be my wife, so yes."

"Not so fast, Thorn. She may be out on her ear if I have my way."

"I'm not too sure about that," Thorn said.

Thorn began to close the door but was interrupted by Edith carrying the tea things. "No thank you, Edith," he said. "Miss Moss will not be here long." He closed the door firmly and faced Clarice. "Phyllida knows everything. She knows about our courtship and our break-up. She even knows about the baby."

Clarice hastily gulped some tea. Why was she so nervous?

"So there is nothing Phyllida doesn't already know? There was a time when you would have never talked with a woman like she were an equal. You used to say how silly women were," she said. "You have changed, Thorn."

Phyllida detected a note of sadness in her voice and she pitied her.

"Tell me about my child."

"You won't see him," she hissed, "until you get rid of her and marry me."

"Tell me about my son," he quietly persisted.

Clarice swallowed. "He's a good boy, very bright and handsome."

Thorn sat at his desk and pulled out the slip of paper. "How old is he?"

Clarice nervously scratched her neck. "He's...he's seventeen."

"What is his name?"

"Why all these questions?" she barked.

"I have a right to ask about my son, don't I?"

Clarice was highly strung now. Thorn leaned his elbows on the desk and said quietly, "There's no child, Clarice."

"Of course there is!"

He shook his head. "I thought you were smarter than this. If we had a son together, at best, he would be sixteen, not seventeen. I'm surprised you didn't do better math. Secondly, I did some checking on you. It's true you married and moved to Detroit after we ended our relationship." He paused to hold up the slip of paper Sandy had given him. "You never had a son...or a daughter for that matter. Sandy telegrammed an investigator in Detroit. Hospital records were checked and it seems our high-society lady never gave birth to a child. I did discover that you had some back trouble," he consulted the list, "but nowhere in the newspapers or in hospital registries does it say you have a child. How do you explain this?"

"I had the child with a midwife in my own home," Clarice said, her face taunt.

"No, you wouldn't have—not being a high-society wife married to one of the most distinguished lawyers in Michigan. It would have been plastered all over the newspapers. I was foolish not to have thought such information would have been published in the newspapers. I never thought to look. I believed you when you came here and implied that I had a child. Guilt made me naive and less skeptical. I've carried guilt all my life, even into my sleep. One night I would dream of a boy, the next a girl. I wrestled and tore myself to shreds wondering, but was too cowardly to act upon my guilt as well as my responsibility. I should have hunted you down and demanded that you tell me about the child. But I was afraid. We sinned, you and I." He paused and looked at Phyllida. "I'm so sorry, Dearest."

Phyllida didn't reply because she didn't trust herself to speak. She felt joy at seeing his true feelings of retribution. He was finally forgiving himself.

"This is nonsense!"

Thorn persisted. "Why did you do this, Clarice? Why did you make up such a story? Did you really think you were pregnant?"

Clarice shrieked, "I lied about the baby! I wasn't pregnant; I never thought I was. I needed you to marry me!" Her face flushed, the anger flashing in her startling green eyes. "I knew I couldn't have children, but I couldn't tell you. I needed to secure a marriage where my father and I would be well taken care of. His debts were mounting and his creditors were bombarding him. We needed to act fast so we attended a high society event and that's when I met you."

"How did you intend to fool me about the pregnancy? Didn't you think I'd eventually wonder?" he asked, raising his eyebrows.

"I planned on having all the ills of a woman in early pregnancy, but then would fake a miscarriage. My father and I already knew of a doctor who, for the right price, would validate my false condition so you'd never question the situation. From there the doctor would inform you that because of my miscarriage, I would never have another child."

"Why did you lie about your ability to conceive?"

"Because," she paused, her eyes tearing, "I couldn't bear to tell you or any man that I was...was less of a woman." She began to weep. "I've spent my life hating myself, all because of one little unfortunate horse riding accident."

"Are you sure?"

"Of course I am!" she hissed. "Would I go to such trouble if the doctors hadn't confirmed this? I am damaged goods. My father knew it too and had to marry me off to someone with money so my father's future and mine was secure. And no man, especially a wealthy one, would settle to marry me, a barren women unable to produce an heir."

"Did Charles know?"

"Ah," she shook her head, "That's where I lucked out. When he proposed, he went on to say that he never wanted children since his were all grown. He hoped I would never become pregnant and because of his illness, he had little to worry about if I had been...normal."

"Clarice." Thorn was pale. Phyllida saw his pity for this proud but hurt woman. "If you had been honest with me from the beginning, perhaps things would have been different."

"Would you have married me had you known of my condition?"

"I would have, yes. But you didn't want me, remember?"

"I was so disappointed at the prospect of living at the Ravines. I was angry with you, Thorn, but later regretted my deception and greed. I wasn't married to Charles a week and I missed you terribly. It was too late. But it's not too late now."

Thorn shook his head and instinctively turned to Phyllida. She looked tired, but she was there for him, waiting until this storm passed, just as she had always promised. "No, Clarice."

"But what about your obligations?" Clarice began to babble. "I have pined for you the last sixteen years. I waited for Charles to die so we could be together again. I realize now what an awful mistake I made. Please, Thorn. Please reconsider."

"I don't know you, Clarice. So many years have passed; you're a stranger to me."

Clarice stood. "But look at me. I'm still pretty. I could throw great parties, entertain business associates... Besides," she paused, "I'm not scarred like she is."

Phyllida's hand instinctively touched her ear and neck where they had become exposed for the world to see. She pulled her long hair around her neck and slowly backed away. Clarice was right, Phyllida thought. She would always be plain, and she had accepted that. However, to be scarred would make her an eyesore, especially when she was at Thorn's side, Thorn who was handsome beyond any physical flaws. She felt embarrassed, and needed to be alone.

"Phyllida, wait!" Thorn called out.

"I shall be fine, Thorn." She braved a smile and closed the door after them, walking briskly past Sandy, Lewis and Veronica who waited in the hallway.

"Where are you going, m'dear?" Veronica whispered.

She went to her room and hastily threw on a long wool cloak. Before Veronica could find her, she slipped out the back stairway and into the night. The cool air nipped at the stream of tears on her cheeks. The stable boys who huddled around the fire jumped up when she walked in.

"May I have a horse, please?"

"Ma'am?"

"I'd like to go riding."

"Have you ever ridden before?"

"A little."

"Then we best saddle up Whisper, she's docile and patient."

When she alighted, the nodded at the bewildered stable boys as Whisper trotted them into the dark night.

"Why did you say such a thing?" Thorn thundered.

"Thorn, it's true. She's scarred, no matter how she tries to pull that hair around her neck. She'll always have a scarred ear and neck. You know how looks are important, especially to a man of your stature. Besides, she's not even that pretty."

"Get out!" he said in a deliberate tone."Get out and never step foot into my home again."

"But what about the ring, and the letter saying you pledged your undying— "

"What kind of threat do you have now? Are you going to the papers with this dim-witted story? You married someone else, no matter what that letter states. You had a chance of happiness with Charles, but you chose not to take it. Now it's my turn." He pounded his chest. "I have made my choice: Phyllida Cowen will be my wife."

"You had to buy her. Oh yes," she hissed, her pleading returned to malice, "I heard how you had to bring her over from England. You had to pay her debts to get her to marry you! All because of your father's will! What a crazy old man!"

He was about to correct her about Phyllida's debts actually being more his own since Ernst was his cousin, but he knew reasoning with Clarice would only lead to more conversation.

"Sandy!" Thorn called. On cue, Sandy came into the library and gently grasped Clarice's elbow. "It is as he says, Clarice. It's over now."

Thorn heard her tirade but he had no time to put a stop to it; Phyllida needed him and nothing else mattered.

After he checked her room, he then made his way to the kitchens where one of the stable boys was drinking hot cider. "She's gone, sir. We saddled up Whisper and she rode away about a half hour ago."

Thorn ran out to the stables. "Get me Firestorm," he commanded of the stable boys. The great black stallion was quickly ushered to Thorn.

"He's kind of feisty tonight, sir."

Ignoring him, Thorn asked, "Which way did Miss Cowen go?"

"Towards the Ravines, sir."

He set off in a wild gallop.

It was past midnight when Phyllida returned.

She led Whisper to the stables and one of the stable boys asked, "Is Mr. Thorn behind you?"

"No, why would he be?"

"Why, he set out right after you."

She rushed to the house.

She met Sandy and Lewis, who asked, "Is he with you?"

"No, I thought he was here."

"He went after you, and we haven't seen him since."

"Oh no!" she said. "Perhaps he followed my tracks to the Ravines."

"He's probably all right, but let's get a search party started," Lewis said, not wanting to mention his concern about the recent cougar sightings. "Thorn knows the woods like the back of his hand." He patted Phyllida's hand reassuringly.

"Even in the dark?" she asked skeptically. She had an uncanny feeling Thorn was far from safe.

Thorn was grateful for the silvery moonlight that filtered through the trees. He followed Whisper's tracks into the Ravines. It was strangely quiet. He called Phyllida's name while Firestorm snorted impatiently. The dense trees made it more difficult to follow her tracks. As he squinted to adjust his eyes to the shadows, he was struck by an eerie silence.

Firestorm began to stir uncomfortably. "Easy boy," he soothed.

What if Phyllida has fallen somewhere? he worried. He felt sure she was here, or had been here. As he turned to head up the steep embankment, he heard a low growl.

Everything happened quickly.

Firestorm reared as the cougar screamed, making its presence known.

Thorn clutched the saddle and cried, "Easy does it, Boy!" But it was too late. Firestorm bolted. The trees whipped past Thorn, some so close that he felt the bark scrape past his legs. Firestorm continued to dodge the trees as Thorn ducked, all the while trying to restrain the frightened animal. His knee scraped past one trunk. *That was close*— he thought, but before he knew it, Firestorm had slid past a large pine with such speed that his knee drove into the tree and he was thrust from the horse. Firestorm ran into the night as Thorn hit the ground with a thud. For a moment, he blinked at the towering pines swaying noiselessly above him. Then he felt the biting pain in his knee. The splintering shards of pain rang through his body and he cried out. He was afraid to look down, but forced his chin to his chest. His leg had been broken and the bone was exposed from the skin. He felt a warm trickle of blood run down the side of his head.

He fell back and was engulfed in blackness.

"Thorn!" Phyllida cried.

The search party consisted of Phyllida, Sandy, Lewis and several stable men. Their lanterns glowed, but their sight was limited due to the clouds that temporarily covered the moonlight. They called his name, even the horse's name, but were answered with their own voices echoing into the far corners of the woods. They broke into groups and continued their search into what seemed the early morning hours. Phyllida prayed for Thorn's return, begging God to forgive her for her hasty action. "It's all my fault," she kept saying. "If I hadn't run out of the house, he would never have— " Her thoughts were interrupted by the sound of galloping hooves. As the search party parted on the little logging trail, they waited, holding their lanterns high.

"Thorn," Sandy called, "is that you?"

Firestorm materialized from the shadows. He looked eerie, his black shiny body emerging from the forest. He snorted impatiently and stomped.

"Oh no!" Phyllida cried. "He's lost! He's been hurt!"

"Don't panic," Sandy said. "Firestorm's come from the west of the Ravines. Thorn's got to be there." He pointed his gun towards the steep embankment.

"Let's go."

One by one, they led their horses down the embankment, each silent as they wondered about the fate of Thorn Langworthy.

Thorn was in and out of consciousness. He had once heard his mother play a lovely song. When he had asked her the name of it, she said it was called "On the Wings of a Song." He felt he was gliding on the wings of a song. He heard voices in hushed whispers discussing the fate of his leg. He also heard a woman's voice singing softly. He could hear himself begging her not to stop, for when she sang, he glided through his childhood. He saw his mother's sweet facing saying, "One day you'll come back to the teachings of your youth." Next he had conversations with his father who said Thorn would make Langworthy Lumber an empire. Then he saw disappointment in his father's face. 'What have I done wrong?" he cried to the sad, withered eyes of his once powerful father. "Why have you forsaken me?" But his father only shook his head, saying, "It was I who disappointed you."

And so his dreams faded into fiction and fantasy. What was real, what was true?

At one point, he awoke to a piercing pain his leg. He thought he heard Sandy say, "It will be over quickly, Brother. Just hold on." It almost made Thorn cry to think of Sandy. He had never given him any credit for standing by him. Instead, he always accused Sandy of jealousy. He was the one who was jealous. He hated Sandy for his sense of peace. Sandy loved God, and Thorn didn't know how to—but he was learning. "I'll never be the man you are, Sandy." To this came the reply, "Just be you, Thorn." But he didn't know who he was anymore.

Lewis found him first.

"He's here! Come quickly!"

They turned their horses in the direction of Lewis's voice. The temperature had risen, causing a slight early morning fog. She could see the outline of Lewis bending over a body, Thorn's body. She nearly choked. "Is he alive?"

"Yes he is, but he's not in good condition," Lewis said.

Phyllida ran to the motionless figure. His face was ashen and damp with perspiration. "He has fever, Sandy. Feel his face."

"That's not all," Sandy said as he examined Thorn's leg. Phyllida nearly fainted when she saw the odd way his leg rested along his body. Then she saw the bone, pink with bloody flesh.

"It's a miracle the cougar didn't finish him off. Look, tracks are everywhere around him!" Lewis said, pointing to the large cat prints outlining Thorn's body.

"Lewis, take one of the stable boys and get Doc," Sandy commanded. "Tell him to meet us at the cottage at the Ravines; Thorn's in no shape to be taken back to Twin Pines."

After they left, Sandy said, "We need to get him out of the cold. He's obviously been lying here for hours and has had long exposure to the elements." They quickly began to assemble a makeshift stretcher using fallen branches and rope that was tied to Sandy's saddle. They used their coats to make bedding.

"This will get him to the cottage," he said. On the same count, they lifted him and rested him into the stretcher. He did not move or flinch, a detail that began to worry Phyllida.

"His head is bleeding, Sandy. We've got to hurry," she said, noticing the fresh blood that trickled around his ear. "I'll walk alongside him." She covered him with her cloak.

"You'll freeze," Sandy warned, also removing his coat for Thorn.

"Don't worry about me, just get us moving."

She tucked their cloaks around him, trying to ignore the strange way his leg rested. As if sensing the urgency and delicacy of Thorn's condition, Sandy's horse began to move steadily. The cot jolted and jiggled as Phyllida held the lantern high. She prayed the cottage would show itself soon.

"What can we do?" she asked Sandy at length.

"We're doing all we can," he said patiently.

"Will he live?"

Sandy didn't answer, but said, "Thorn once told me that you had the most beautiful voice he had ever heard. So please, sing and let Thorn hear you."

She began to sing, her voice softly echoing into the pale wintry morning.

Thorn heard Lewis say, "Brother, it's me, Lewis. Can you hear me?" Thorn wanted to reply, "Yes!" but his words were frozen, and his thoughts jumbled. He hated himself for neglecting his brother over the years.

In his blurred thoughts he asked Lewis, "Why do you admire me so?"

"Because I love you like a father. You were always more approachable than Papa. I wanted to be like you in so many ways."

"Why me?"

"Why not?" came the reply. Thorn drifted further into darkness, the image of Lewis fading.

Phyllida would not leave his side.

Because of his injuries, Doc Armstrong said he should stay at the cottage by the Ravines until he could be safely moved. Phyllida agreed and asked that her clothes and Bible be brought to the cottage. Edith sent her things along with a large basket of food, candles, kerosene and an ample water supply. Despite the doctor's concerns that she too rest, she refused to leave. Lewis and Sandy came and went, each taking shifts to stay with Phyllida and Thorn.

It was the longest two weeks of Phyllida's life.

She slept very little, bathing behind a sheet she had hung in a corner. Often she discovered nervous energy and went about sweeping and dusting the cottage. It hadn't been used in years, but with the sunlight of the day, she worked while watching Thorn. Doc continued to check his progress but said little other than, "He's had a concussion. His breathing is normal, but I don't know the fate of his leg."

Lewis had helped the doctor set his leg. It was a horrible moment, but she refused to be ill and turn away. She wasn't a weakling; in fact, she steadied his shoulders and stroked his head as the men prepared. "You'll hear a crack. Just hold him steady. If this doesn't wake him up, I don't know what will."

Sandy bent over the unconscious Thorn, saying, "It will be over quickly, Brother. Just hold on."

The sickening crack and pop nearly sent Lewis outside to vomit. For a moment Thorn's eyes opened, but they closed again immediately.

"He's fighting a terrible fever. Give him a dose of this," he handed Phyllida a bottle, "and keep him cooled off. The fever will break soon. If not, we'll need to get him to a hospital. Charlie Baker's wife is ready to birth their fourth child, so I best be off. I'll return to check on him as soon as mother and baby are fine," he said, kindly patting Phyllida's shoulder.

When Lewis and Doc left, darkness seemed to settle in quickly. Sandy was sleeping in a chair close by, but Phyllida continued her vigil. She sang while embroidering a pillow she knew she would never finish, as it would remind her of this tumultuous time. She glanced constantly at Thorn who seemed to sleep fitfully. Sandy, who had awakened, walked over and asked Thorn, "How are you, Brother?"

Thorn seemed to hear him and began babbling about how he was sorry for doing Sandy wrong and for being jealous of him. Sandy hushed him saying, "All is well, Brother. You're a good man."

"I am not the man you are," he mumbled.

"I don't know what this all means," Phyllida said.

"He's battling right now," Sandy said. He needs to fight his ghosts."

Frank told Davis, "It's all over. Forget everything."

"What?"

"The word in town is that Thorn and his fiancée are missing. There was a big to-do at the Pines on the night of the winter social. From what I hear, she left the house in a hurry and Thorn followed. They haven't been seen since and no one from the house is talking."

Davis scratched his head. "Do you think they're dead?"

"I don't know, and I don't care. Let's forget them and get out of here."

"Not so fast. Let's keep an eye on Twin Pines."

"It's not worth it anymore."

"Are you backing out on me?" He flashed Frank a dark stare.

"Brothers stick together, but this is getting to be too much."

"Don't be a coward. Let's just do some looking around at the Pines."

Phyllida asked Sandy to leave a little early so she could bathe.

"Of course," he replied, glancing at his watch. "Lewis should be here within a half hour. Are you sure you'll be all right by yourself?"

She nodded, already pouring hot water into the hip bath.

She waved him off, drew the curtains on the windows, pulled the sheet across the bath and enjoyed a refreshing but quick soak. She dressed and brushed out her hair, pausing to check on Thorn, who was still fighting delirium as he mumbled and jerked in his sleep. She was about to go outside to dispose of the bath water.

Something piqued her senses. She listened intently.

She heard the sound of footsteps in the snow. Judging by the pattern of the steps, she realized there was more than one person outside. She doubted one of them was Lewis. The steps seemed to slow, becoming more quiet and deliberate. She waited, her heart pounding. She was grateful that the curtains were drawn across the windows. She blew out the lantern and quickly grabbed the loaded rifle that rested beside the door.

Phyllida quietly pulled the cock and waited, her back against the wall. She felt the pine logs scratching through her gown as the steps drew closer to the door. She wished she could quiet Thorn as she sensed someone paused outside the door listening. She crept closer and heard faint breathing on the other side. As she reached the door to ensure it was locked, she felt the pressure on the other side of the handle as someone began to depress the lock.

She aimed the gun and waited.

The lock clicked and the door slowly opened. Phyllida gently touched the trigger of the gun and said quietly, "If you open that door any further, I will blow a hole into your body."

She was surprised by the seriousness of her threat, but she spoke from the heart. No one would harm Thorn, not if she could help it.

The door froze in place. She squinted, trying to make out the figures of the two men who watched her from the doorway. The flicker from the fire sent deceptive shadows around the room and she could not fathom their faces.

But she saw the whites of their eyes.

They seemed to wait, almost as if they were assessing the seriousness of her threat. Reading their thoughts, Phyllida aimed the gun and stepped closer. "You have three seconds to move off my threshold."

"Let's go," one whispered.

"You won't shoot," the other said. "You're just a little skiff of a gal. If we stand here long enough, you'll have to drop that heavy gun."

"If you stand here long enough, your friend will have to drag your body home."

The one turned on his heel and ran while the other stood in place. "You don't scare me, little lady. I'll catch up with you. Just you wait." He turned his back on her before letting the door close behind them.

She rushed to the door and locked it, placing a chair beneath the doorknob. Then turning to Thorn, she murmured, "That was close, Dearest."

She was answered with incoherent words.

"Come back to us soon, Thorn," she said, leaning wearily against the door.

Chapter 8

Thorn seemed suspended for days, months and years and hinged on nothing, but he temporarily surfaced to see images. Somewhere in the darkness the voice continued to sing lovingly. How he tried to reach the voice! He pushed past memories, some faded, some vibrant, but still he could not touch the voice that paused to take a breath and sing on. Then he remembered his mother's words: "Faith is the bird that sings while it is dark."

"What does that mean?" he asked.

"The bird knows that light will come and though it's dark and ominous all around him, he just knows that light will come. Remember, this too shall pass."

"Faith is the bird that sings while it is dark," he repeated out loud. His own voice interrupted his consciousness, and reality, a far off friend, returned.

The ever-present singing paused, "Thorn?"

Phyllida! He tried to blink. Phyllida, the girl, the woman, all that he wanted in life was close by. He opened his eyes and saw her hands, the way her nails were sensibly rounded. He saw her soft mouth and her wide, glowing smile. Her dark eyes gazed at him through her tears. "Thorn, have you come back to me? Shall I sing some more?" She began to sing again, something about how great God was, peace like a river...he opened his eyes, but reality still hadn't registered.

There she sat by his side wearing a pale yellow cotton gown, the neckline showing her slender neck. He saw the scar along her neck and ear, and on her ears she wore her beloved pearls. How ironic that though the flesh had been seared and bore the angry marks of pain, a small, perfect pearl shone brightly in the morning light. Her hair was pulled back and his eyes slowly traveled over her face.

"Have you come home to me?"

He nodded, his own voice sounding strangely happy. "I'm home, Phyllida. I'm home now."

Thorn was able to sit up.

"How long was I unconscious?"

"Two weeks and one day," Phyllida said.

"Were you frightened?" he asked, noting the tired smudges under her eyes.

"Terribly, but the Lord watched over you. I just helped a little."

"Tell me what happened."

Phyllida started from the beginning when she had hastily left Clarice and Thorn in the library. "I just wanted to be alone. I suppose in many ways I had been fighting my own pride and vanity. The scars bothered me more than I realized and when I saw Clarice, with her beauty and style, I suppose I felt all the more wounded when she attacked the way I looked. After you left to chase me," she said, glancing at him apologetically, "Sandy ushered Clarice into town. She was advised to take the next morning's train and never to return."

"She went without a fight?"

"Sandy said she seemed defeated, but there was nothing more she could do."

"I feel sorry for the way I spoke to her."

"I'd rather you feel pity for her than anger and resentment. It would be difficult not to be able to have children, but God compensates for such losses. I wish her some kind of happiness, though it's up to her to obtain it."

He was quiet for a moment, and then said, "Tell me how you all found me."

She told the tale from finding his unconscious body in the Ravines and the cougar tracks around his body. "Why the animal chose not harm you, I have no idea." She went on to tell him how he was brought to the cottage. "But then we had night visitors," she said, telling him about the two men who had come to the door.

Thorn looked alarmed. "What did you do?"

She said quite seriously, "I aimed a gun at them and threatened to put a hole into their bodies."

"No, not you!" He stared incredulously.

"Indeed, I would have."

"To protect me?"

She nodded, then rushed on, "Lewis and one of the stable boys arrived within the hour. When I told him what had happened, we agreed that it was best that we bring you home. It was a risk considering the state of your health, but it wasn't wise to stay any longer. At least we're safer at home."

"Do you really feel this is home?"

She nodded. "Always."

Thorn fidgeted. "I need to get my clothes on."

"Why?" she pressed him back.

"I can't let those Cleary boys get to you. They obviously mean business."

"You must rest. Besides, I'm not even sure it was the Cleary Brothers."

"What if they had hurt you?"

"I had the gun— "

"It doesn't matter. They could have set fire to the cottage just like they did to the office…"

She pressed her finger to his lips. "We have bigger fish to fry."

He laughed. "You're adapting to American linguistics very nicely. What do you have planned?"

"Why, we have a wedding to organize!" She smiled.

"Phyllida," he said quite seriously, "what about my leg? I won't be able to walk like most men. Doc says I'll always use a cane."

"What a pair we'll make with your leg and my scars!" She laughed.

"Will we always laugh at such catastrophes?" He smiled, relieved.

"This is a catastrophe?" She pointed at his leg wrapped in a cast. "You could have lost your leg altogether like the war veterans we see in town. No, this is not a catastrophe, just an adjustment."

He caressed her hair as it fell in heavy long curls around her neck and shoulders. She was beautiful in an unearthly way. Her porcelain features, emphasized by her dark eyes, glowed with life and passion.

"Did you sing to me while I was ill?"

"Why, yes."

"I was comforted by your voice, Phyllida. I was so blinded by the darkness as I struggled to find some sort of reality. When you sang, I found myself clinging to the sound as if it were leading me somewhere. Your voice confirmed that I was alive. Somewhere in the blur of it all, I remembered something my mother said: 'Faith is the bird that sings while it is dark.' I had forgotten this as I became more self-absorbed. Then, before my father died, he told me, 'Find the bird that sings while it is dark.' That little bird is you—you sang in my darkness, bringing to me hymns of the faith, words of hope and promise…" He paused. "…and God brought her to me. I hope you never fly away."

The wedding was quiet and discreet.

Pastor Linden married Thorn and Phyllida while their guests—Lewis, Veronica, Irving, Edith, and her daughters—watched. Ruby stood as Phyllida's maid of honor, while Sandy stood in as best man. Phyllida's dress, a white muslin gown, fit her form nicely, emphasizing her beauty without heavy garnish and beadwork. Her hair, held back by a small band of white silk flowers, sent her rich hair falling in large ringlets down her back. Her only jewelry, the small pearl earrings, adorned each ear. Thorn's heart raced as he slid the small gold band on her finger. He had encouraged her to wear the large diamond that had belonged to his mother, but she declined saying, "A gold band is all that I want."

He respected her wishes and actually preferred the warm gleam of the gold to the cold glitter of diamonds. When the rings were exchanged, Pastor Linden said, "You may kiss your bride."

He leaned down, grasping each of her hands in his own and kissing her lightly. But before withdrawing, he impulsively slid his arms around her waist and held her. For a moment, no one spoke as he held her like his friend and his lover. At length he whispered, "Thank you, Philly, for being my wife." Never before had he known such a true sense of love, friendship and appreciation.

She echoed his sentiments, murmuring "God is good" and resting her cheek against his. Though they had known each other just a few short months, their paths, becoming one, had been tumultuous. For a quiet moment, they felt joy and the relief knowing that they could put the past behind them.

They turned to receive their guests' hugs and hearty handshakes.

Pastor Linden shook Thorn's hand. "Will I be seeing you more often?"

Thorn laughed. "Probably more than you'd like."

"Thanks for the warning." The Pastor laughed, slapping Thorn's arm.

Thorn turned to Sandy, who also shook his hand. "Brother, your life turned out better than I ever imagined."

"Thank you for everything, Sandy."

"What are brothers for?"

Lewis hugged Phyllida, then turned to Thorn. "I know you don't like hugging, so let me just say—"

He was unprepared for the embrace from Thorn. "I'm proud of you, Lewis. You've done well for yourself."

Lewis smiled, not trusting himself to speak. He turned to motion to Irving Hamilton, who was waiting his turn to congratulate Thorn. He shook his hand. "I know I wasn't exactly invited, but I had to see you two wed. Nothing has pleased me more."

"We used to be good friends, didn't we?"

"Sure," Irving said, slightly perplexed.

"Let's start again, Irv."

Irving nodded, grinning. Then, turning to Phyllida he said, "I don't know who's happier, Thorn or me."

"What do you mean?" she asked.

"Ruby and I are going to be married."

"How wonderful! Congratulations!" She hugged Ruby who was brushing a tear off her face.

"He decided that he don't mind me bein' a big time business lady after all." She smiled as Irving turned her hand over to kiss it. She nudged him. "Tell 'em, Irv."

"Tell us what?"

"There are some visitors waiting for you outside."

"Who?"

"Just follow me." Irving winked at Phyllida and Thorn.

The wedding party stepped outside into the January air. Once their gazes had adjusted to the glare from the sun radiating off the snow, Thorn let out a shout. "What is this?" For across the lawn of Twin Pines, nearly three hundred men stood and waved their winter caps, shouting their congratulations. Irving motioned them to move together to assemble a sort of choir. To Thorn and Phyllida's delight, the lumberjacks sang, their voices in harmony. Phyllida marveled at the deep baritones, altos, and tenors. When finished, they raised their arms in applause.

Irving turned to Thorn. "They have been practicing all the way here. They've come from miles to be here to wish you well."

"This calls for a celebration!" Thorn called, waving them inside.

Edith, who was always one step ahead of him, gathered the servants to set place settings throughout the ballroom. Hot coffee and tea was on the way while the cooks, who had known in advance of the gathering, put the finishing touches on honey-glazed ham, homemade bread and apple pie.

"I never imagined my wedding would be so large after all!" Phyllida laughed as she greeted the men. They entered the foyer in threes and fours, and soon the house was full of lumberjacks.

They didn't notice the two men who slipped past the ballroom and went upstairs.

While the lumberjacks enjoyed heir hearty meals, Thorn summoned his brothers to the library where he produced a sheet of paper from his desk.

"What's this all about, Brother?" Sandy asked.

Phyllida stood next to Thorn, barely able to contain her excitement.

"As you know, I've married in time to fulfill Father's obligations. But that's not why I married her," he said, gazing down Phyllida. "Anyway, the land, company and house are intact. But there have been a few changes."

Lewis and Sandy glanced at each other.

"We've already decided to move," Lewis spoke up. "We thought you'd need the place to yourself now that you're married."

"That's not necessary," Phyllida said.

"We plan on living at the cottage," Thorn said, handing them the sheet of paper. "This is a deed to the company. I no longer own Langworthy Lumber."

"What?"

"It's owned by Thornton, Sanford, and Lewis Langworthy. The entire business is to be owned and operated in thirds."

"Thorn," Sandy began, "we didn't expect this!"

"You two will manage the company, as I will be working for you now."

"But we didn't expect you— " Sandy began, but Thorn put up his hand.

"It's the least I can do. The house is ours as well, not just mine."

Lewis leaned over and whispered something to Sandy. He nodded and looked up. "We're very flattered, Thorn. In fact, I'm touched that you should think so highly of us. And we gladly accept…on one condition."

Thorn raised his eyebrows.

"You and Phyllida will remain at Twin Pines, and Lewis and I will build our own homes. It was always a dream of ours to design our own places, just as Papa did. We hope to one day have wives and families to share them with."

"Are you sure?" Phyllida asked.

They nodded and Thorn thanked them with a firm handshake.

The festivities continued into the night involving fiddle duets, banjo solos, and story telling. Thorn and Phyllida laughed and clapped while Lewis and Sandy reacquainted themselves with their employees. At length Sandy said, "You may want to hear some of the jacks' ideas."

Thorn raised his hand. "It's all yours now, Brother."

He felt good saying that as he was tired of the years of hoarding and obsessing over the business. Phyllida squeezed his hand. "You did the right thing."

"It should have been done a long time ago."

She stifled a yawn. "I think I'll go upstairs and change out of this dress."

He kissed her lightly, his warm gaze assessing her face and the question in her eyes. "Shall I come with you?"

"Give me an half an hour to bathe," she replied.

"Thirty minutes and counting." He winked.

She smiled and rose, bidding the jacks farewell. Meeting Edith in the hallway, she thanked her for the lovely dinner.

Edith asked, "Can I get you anything, ma'am?"

"I'd love a warm bath."

"I'll send Bella promptly."

Phyllida made her way up the winding staircase, pausing to glance at the portrait of old Mr. Langworthy. She regarded him for a moment, his eyes seeming lifelike. This man, she mused, lived to build a great fortune, but in the end couldn't take any of it with him. "Life is fleeting," she murmured, "but the treasures built in heaven are forever."

She stepped into the corridor and noticed the hall lanterns were unlit. She blindly felt the walls and finally reached Thorn's room. She paused to fumble for a match by the bedside and lit a candle. Phyllida paused to gaze around her new bedroom, and also to notice the large amount of dried flowers and wedding presents stacked on the table, near the foot of the bed. She read some of the cards, smiling at the thoughtful words written by some of the lumberjack's wives, Ruby, and even from Maisy and Betty. Still waiting for Bella to bring the water, Phyllida loitered over by the wardrobe where Edith had hung her gowns.

She opened the door and drew a breath to scream.

Davis Cleary covered her mouth and whispered, "I told you we'd meet again."

Thorn was saying good-bye to several lumberjacks when Bella whispered, "Sir, may I have a word with you?" Without waiting for an answer, she grasped his arm. "I found this note on the bed. She's gone, sir. She disappeared into thin air!"

His eyes quickly scanned the poorly written note which warned that Thorn must leave $5,000 in the crook of Pine Knob tree, or Phyllida's life would be ended: "Don't doubt me, or you'll find her dead in the river."

Pine Knob stood on the outskirts of town along the clearing of the Au Sable River. Pine Knob was a large, old tree that had spilt and grown into two different directions. He remembered it as being a fine tree to climb as a child

"Bella, gather as many men as you can and have them meet me in the stables!" With his cane, he limped to the library and opened the large gun cabinet in the corner.

Sandy appeared, asking, "What is it, Thorn? What is Bella in a fit about?"

Thorn handed him the note followed by a loaded rifle. "My wife," he began and swallowed, "my wife has been taken—kidnapped! Dress up!"

The men quickly dressed as Edith and Bella rushed from the kitchens carrying full lanterns. Lewis, following them out to the stables, carried loaded rifles for the search party. Thorn hurried to his stallion, wincing from the pain in his leg. He ignored the hint of embarrassment as the stable boys helped him onto his horse. Thorn looked over the lumberjacks, nearly ten of them, who were volunteering their help. Sandy, Lewis and Irving also accompanied him, each holding their lanterns high and waiting for Thorn's directions.

"Does everyone have a loaded weapon?"

He was answered with affirmations. He glanced at Edith and Bella who stood aside, wrapped in shawls and looking very worried.

"It is likely that the Cleary Brothers are behind this," began Thorn. "No matter what, we must bring Phyllida home alive. I'll pay whatever they want and more to see her home safely. However, I also want these men brought to justice.

"Let us have a brief word of prayer," Thorn said as he prayed earnestly for Phyllida's safety, as well as the focus and self-control he would need to not let his anger take over. He knew that his temper was at the killing point, and without God's help, he might do something regretful. "Let us not make hasty judgments, but be thoughtful while protecting ourselves…"

After several hearty amens, Thorn commanded, "Sandy and Irv, head into town and get the sheriff. Lewis and the others, come with me."

Her wedding gown was muddied. She had been drug through the snow and then tossed up on a horse. She shivered, wearing only the thin material, and her breathing was raspy from the cloth stuffed in her mouth. Frank, the younger brother, glanced at her apologetically. "No silly stuff, you hear?"

She nodded as Davis hissed, "Don't talk to her!"

They made their way to the heart of the woods. She had never been on this particular trail before and she prayed that their tracks would be followed. As if reading her thoughts, Davis said, "Don't get too confident, Miss. These tracks could be anybody's. With all the lumberjacks here today, they wouldn't know where to start to follow us." He was right, she thought. How could she be found? She saw that the trail led them around the outskirts of town to a small tar-paper shack.

"When is Pa due back?" Frank asked.

"He'll be at Ruby's until midnight, then over to Monk's Saloon for a spell. By then, he'll come home so spiced he won't know she's here."

"What if he comes home early?"

"He never does and you know it, so hush up and move."

Frank helped her alight the horse, but her heel got caught in the stirrups. He paused to wrestle her foot out of the strap when Davis unexpectedly grabbed her arm and threw her into the cottage, twisting her ankle in the process. "Why are you fussing over her? Do you want to be seen or something?"

She lay on the floor groaning.

"I think you hurt her."

Frank kneeled over her and Davis growled, "Leave her be. Now get a fire going! I'm going to make sure we weren't followed." Davis shut the door behind him and Frank lit a candle, illuminating the dirty shack consisting of three beds, a rustic table and chairs.

After a fire sparked and began to warm them, Frank helped her up and led her to a chair before the fire. "Just do as he says," he whispered. "If your husband delivers the money to Pine Knob, you'll be home by tomorrow…I hope."

"Why are you doing this?" she asked as he pulled the cloth out of her mouth.

"He's my brother," he said, almost pleading.

"But you'll go to jail for this too."

"Just be quiet so I don't have to put this thing back in your mouth, okay?"

She nodded, ignoring the pain in her ankle as he tied her arms to the chair. Davis joined them moments later. "I don't think we were followed. Why isn't her mouth covered?"

"She won't talk," Frank said.

Davis walked slowly towards Phyllida and leaned over her. He tilted her chin upwards so they faced each other. "You're not so tough now, little lady. You still want to blow a hole in my guts?"

"If I had a gun, yes," she said and he raised his hand to slap her.

"Don't do it, Davis," Frank said. "We're in it for the money, nothing more."

Davis pointed a finger at her nose. "If you talk again, I'll tear that tongue out of your throat."

Then Davis turned quickly. "I hear footsteps on the path!" he whispered as he covered Phyllida's mouth. "Someone's coming!"

Frank looked out the window. "It's Pa! He's home! I thought you said he wasn't going to be home this early!"

"I'll take him to the saloon," Davis said as he slowly moved his hand from Phyllida's mouth whispering, "Not a word, little lady. If he hears you, I'll kill you."

Wisely, she did not reply and was relieved when he met his father at the door saying, "Hey, Pa. I was just going out to Monk's. Why don't you join me?"

"Where'd you get the money?" she heard his father ask.

"I got paid today," he said. "Drinks are on me."

He heard the men turn away, their footsteps fading into the night.

Frank sighed, "That was close."

"Your father has no idea what you and your brother are doing?"

"Of course not," Frank said. "He's a drunk but not a kidnapper."

"Why are you doing this? What did I ever do to you?"

"Shhhh," he said, listening. "Let me make sure they're gone."

He rose and went to the window and watched for a few minutes as if contemplating his own plan.

"I've let things go too far. We need to get you out of here." He untied her hands. "I'll take you home; as for me, this is my chance to get away from my brother."

"No, come with me, Frank. Let me explain to Thorn that you helped me."

"They won't believe you. They'll think I put you up to it."

They rushed outside and jumped on the horses. "Just ride fast, Miss. I'll see you to Twin Pines road, but from there, I'll be off on my own."

"Please follow me home. I want you to be there when I tell them the truth."

"No time for talk, Miss. Just move!"

She thrust the horse into a wild gallop and rode towards Twin Pines. She ignored the freezing air biting into her skin. She glanced behind her and saw that Frank was still following. Up ahead, lanterns and approaching horsemen caught her attention.

To her joy, she saw Thorn and raised her arm. "Thorn!"

Lewis, who had stopped his horse, raised his rifle, shouting, "Duck, Phyllida!"

"No! Wait! He's with me!"

But shots rang into the night.

He had never been more surprised than when he saw Phyllida advancing with Frank Cleary behind her. Her hair was loose and wild, her dress torn and muddied. He saw that she was frigid as she raised her arm. Lewis, not understanding what was happening, thought Frank was pursuing Phyllida. Phyllida cried out, but Lewis did not hear.

He shot Frank, and Frank fell with a sickening thud.

She reared the horse and rushed to Frank's side. "He's still breathing. Quick! Get him home. I'll explain everything!"

"Where's Davis?" Thorn asked.

"He's with his father at the saloon. His father knows nothing of this, and should not be arrested," she said before turning her attention to the unconscious Frank.

After the men had laid Frank across the horse, Thorn said, "Lewis, you and the others arrest Davis Cleary, but no harm should come to him or his father."

Frank survived despite a great deal of blood loss. While he recuperated under lock and key in a guest bedroom, Thorn made arrangements that Frank take his father to live in Bay City. Through one of Thorn's associates, Frank would work in a lumber mill while caring for his father. "That way, he can provide for his father, but can be no threat to us."

"He saved my life," Phyllida said, gently defending him.

"But not without jeopardizing your life first. He will be given a chance to begin again, but at a safe distance."

Phyllida did not argue. When she told Frank the good news he smiled, wincing slightly from the pain. "I deserve jail, but you good people are giving me and Pa a new life."

"Make the Lord foremost in your life, Frank. Everything else will fall into place," she said gently.

At length Frank asked, "What about Davis? What happened to him?"

Phyllida explained that he had been promptly arrested for attempted murder, arson and kidnapping. "He'll have a life behind bars, but at least the prison isn't far from Bay City."

He thought for a moment. "Sometimes I wonder what gets the best of us. My ma and pa never taught us to steal, much less swear. Somewhere along the line, we got blinded by all the wrong things."

"In your case, you quit while you were ahead, though it was close. Not stopping your brother's actions almost makes you an accomplice to his crimes."

Frank said, "I'm sorry for all the grief me and my brother caused."

Phyllida squeezed his hand and stood. She was about to leave when Frank asked, "Do you reckon I'll find myself a nice gal like you in Bay City?"

"To find a nice gal, you must be a nice man." She winked. "I believe in the best in you, Frank, but you must prove that to yourself." Despite his pain, Frank would begin again and the years seemed to erase from his face so that, for the first time, he looked and felt young.

Epilogue

December, 1877

Thorn and Phyllida finished their morning run on Firestorm and Whisper. They stepped out of the stables and into the winter sunshine. She glanced up at Twin Pines, seeing the figure of their little boy waving at them with excitement. She waved back. "It looks like they're awake now."

When they reached the front door, Edith took their cloaks and smiled. "The children are chomping at the bit to open presents."

When she left to get them, Thorn said, "It seems like just yesterday we were married. Now we're having Christmas with our little— "

With a shout and a wave, their four-year-old son Edward dashed down the stairs, hugging his mother's leg, then pausing to look dignified. He held out his little hand to his father. "Hello, Papa."

Thorn bowed. "Why, hello Edward. How is my boy?"

"Fine," he said, but the excitement soon burst out. "We want to open presents! Please!"

"Run along to the library, we'll be there shortly."

Thorn laughed and turned to see Jenna. "There's my little fledgling." Their toddler was on her belly and sliding down the steps only to dash after her brother, her little chubby legs trying to keep up.

Phyllida laughed as Thorn murmured, "Do you ever wonder why we are so blessed?"

"By God's grace," she said, then kissed Thorn with the passion she was never without. "Merry Christmas, Dearest."

Her arms reached around his neck. "Let's always keep it this simple."

"We've learned a lot about ourselves, haven't we?"

"I don't think we'll ever stop learning."

They made their way to the library where a cheery fire greeted them. Edward and Jenna were shaking presents and squealing with excitement. Edward, a small dark version of his father, smiled. "Papa, I know what this one is."

"We'll soon find out if your guess is right," Thorn said.

Jenna made her way to her father's lap and he picked her up, holding her little chubby body. "She has my mother's smile and your lovely eyes," he said to Phyllida. She caressed her daughter's small, round face as Thorn led the family in a word of prayer before the gift opening began. Phyllida was mesmerized by the joy of her children, their laughter, the way their faces lit with surprise when they uncovered their small treasures. At length, she turned back to Thorn and found he was watching her with the gaze that always warmed her heart.

"What is it, Dearest?" she asked softly.

"Philly, you seem to float like a bird. I wonder when you take flight, what will you do next?"

"I will return to you…every time," she said with confidence.

-The End-

Printed in the United States
33199LVS00002B/181

9 781413 752328